Protecting

Her

Heart

~A NOVEL~

Elizabeth James

Solitaire Series

Book #2

Edited by Kathy Krick

Cover Design by
ShamRock Cover Designs ©2015

Dedication

As always to Sissy and Bobby...you are always in my heart....with all my love

Thank you

As always, I want to thank my husband and family for their love and support.

Kassie Baker, thank you again for being a part of my crazy book world. You're so tuned in to me that it's scary sometimes...

Kathy Krick, your keen editor's eye and support as my friend have been invaluable to me...I love ya!

Rochelle, you see inside my head and make my covers come to life! Thank you again for your amazing talent.

Thanks to my betas, Kassie Baker, Sharon Courtney, Becky Nichols, Maria DeSouza and

Rochelle McGrath for taking the time to read and let me have your honest feedback.

To my fellow authors and fans I say thank you from the bottom of my heart. You've made this experience unforgettable.

To my E. James Street Team, thank you for all of our pimpin'! You all mean the world to me!!!

Prologue

Ryanne

The room was cold and dark, the only light coming from the monitor by my bedside. The technician, Sara, carefully applied the cold gel to my swollen belly. As she began to slide the probe slowly across my skin, the images began to flicker onto the screen. I watched fascinated as our child moved around, and I instinctively tightened my grip on Rusty's hand. "It never ceases to amaze me," I whispered.

I heard a sniffle and turned my head slightly in time to catch my husband quickly wiping a tear from his eye. "It's pretty great," he said softly.

Sara then began to take some measurements to determine if the baby was growing normally. I was apprehensive about this part, but soon, she nodded slightly and said, "Looks good."

"Does it look like my due date is pretty accurate?" I asked, still watching the screen closely.

She leaned over and consulted my chart. "Yes, it looks like you're going to be pretty close. You're about nineteen weeks now and Dr. Han has your due date around July fourth. I'd say just don't make any big plans around that time," she said laughing.

I looked over at Rusty. "Sweetie, this is going to mess up your schedule, isn't it?" One of the biggest races of the year for Rusty was always held on July fourth.

He shook his head with a smile. "Nope, if you're having that baby, I'll definitely find a backup driver to race for me." Rusty's career as a race car driver was very important to him and despite our best efforts to plan the baby in his off-season, nature had its own way.

Sara continued her measurements and making notes on the computer. "So, Ryanne, I read that you're going to be filming a movie in a few months. I hope you're not going to overdo it."

I shook my head. "No, I've already talked to the director and he totally understands my situation. Luckily for me, the character I'll be playing is a pregnant woman. It's a really short shooting schedule anyway."

Rusty brushed my cheek with the back of his hand. "I'm not really happy about this movie thing but I also trust her to take care of herself."

She nodded. "Are you taking Gage with you?" she asked.

"Yes, I'll be traveling with my assistant Kimberly and an amazing nanny who'll help with him, and of course I'll have my security with me too."

Sara fanned herself. "Do you mean Mason? He's so yummy!"

I laughed out loud. "Yes, Mason will be going." Mason Leffler, my personal bodyguard, had come with me to most of my appointments as my protection from zealous photographers. Since news had broken about my pregnancy, the tabloid's interest in me had increased so it was safer to have him with me. Apparently, he was pretty popular with the staff. At six foot three with long dark hair that he kept tied back, he was an imposing figure but in reality, he was a real sweet guy.

Sara smiled. "So, do you want to know what you're having?"

Rusty and I answered simultaneously.

"No," I said emphatically.

"Yes!" he said nodding his head vigorously.

Sara laughed then put her hands on her hips. "Well, we have a dilemma. From the ultrasound, I can tell the sex of the baby but now I need to know what to do next."

Rusty's face fell and he looked so disappointed that I had to give in. "Well, since Rusty wants to know, go ahead and tell us. I just really wanted it to be a surprise."

He took my hand and brought my fingertips to his lips. "Baby, if you want to wait, then I can wait. I promise, it'll be fine."

I thought for a moment then had an idea. "Sara, could you just write it down and slip it into an envelope. We'll figure out what to do later."

Rusty smiled. "That sounds like a plan!" He turned to Sara and said, "My wife, what can I say…she's pretty awesome."

4

Sara nodded in agreement with a smile. "She certainly is." She pulled a piece of paper from a drawer and turning her back to us, wrote down the sex of our baby. She slipped it into a plain white envelope and handed it to Rusty. "Here you go. I'll print some pictures that don't give the results away so you can show your family."

Rusty took the envelope, folded it, and slipped it into his pocket. Sara printed several pictures and handed them to me in a long roll. The image was so vivid, every detail so clear, and I was thankful we'd gone with the newest ultrasound. Rusty and I huddled together admiring the pictures while Sara cleaned me up.

"That's a good-lookin' kid," Rusty said with a wink. "I have a feeling it's gonna be a girl just as pretty as her mama." He leaned in to kiss my forehead. "I can't wait to meet our little miracle."

I looked up at my handsome husband with a tear in my eye and whispered, "I love you." He kissed me softly on the lips then rested his forehead against mine.

Chapter 1

Mason

"Ryanne, you have five minutes before we have to leave," I called out as I knocked on the door to her suite.

"Dammit!" She yelled. "I can't find my shoe! Mason, can you help me?"

I slowly eased the door open and saw Ryanne holding a sandal with a bright yellow sunflower on it. "Gage must've been playing with my stuff again because I can't find the match to this shoe. Plus, I can't get down on the floor to look under the bed."

I got down on my knees and pulled up the bedspread. Reaching under, I pulled out some plastic building blocks, half of a peanut butter sandwich, and the missing shoe. Ryanne shook her head and laughed. "I swear that boy is a mess!"

Climbing to my feet, I laughed and nodded in agreement. "Yeah, last week he took Mrs. Jamison's phone and put it in the freezer. We finally found it and luckily, it still works."

Ryanne sighed. "I'm so sorry. He's such a handful and with me being almost eight months pregnant, he thinks he can get away with even more. I'm not quick like I used to be."

I checked my watch. "Well, you'd better be quick because we literally have to leave right now. Ms. Rafe's already in the car waiting."

She leaned on me as she slipped her sandals on, grabbed her purse and keys and we headed out the door. She was scheduled to film a scene in downtown Wilmington at the waterfront and luckily we were only a few blocks away. Coming out the front of the hotel, I cleared a path for her through the crowd amidst flashes from cameras and fans telling her they loved her. Using my hand for support, she slid into the back seat of the SUV and I swiftly shut the door. I quickly jumped into the driver's seat and pulled away from the curb.

I glanced in the mirror and watched as she applied some touch ups to her makeup as she and her assistant went over her schedule. Ryanne was gorgeous and the pregnancy had only enhanced her beauty. Despite the fact she was a married woman, I couldn't help but admire her. Any man would be a fool not to notice. What I loved most was how normal she was in a world full of pretentious actors. She was so considerate, always asking me how I was doing, always remembered my birthday and could read me like a book when I was having a good or bad day. We'd grown close since Ryder had assigned her to me and I was very thankful he had. At first, Gage had shied away from me and Ryder had been tempted to assign Joey to them but I was patient and persistent and he soon lost his shyness around me.

I really enjoyed being around her son. He was adorable and made me long to have a child of my own. Unfortunately, he also reminded me of one of the reasons why my marriage had failed. In reality, several things had killed my marriage but one of the main things was that I wanted kids and my wife, Kristin, didn't. Our relationship didn't start out that way. We'd started dating in college and the entire time we dated, she talked about the future and how she wanted at least four kids, two boys and two girls. Once we got married, things quickly changed. She began to use the excuse that she was too busy with her career as a physician's assistant. One day, after a particularly ugly fight, I just came out and asked her if she ever intended to start a family with me and she crushed me when she made it clear that wasn't ever going to be a possibility.

From that day on, I became the most dedicated cop in LA, working overtime any chance I could get to avoid going home. Late one night, after taking an armed robbery call, I ended up in the middle of a shootout with the suspect and got hit by a round in the shoulder. I was sent to the closest hospital which happened to be where she was supposed to be working. It turned out that she wasn't. In fact, she'd been working a different shift for several months. After my release from the hospital, I had one of my fellow officers drive me home, and I sat in my recliner angrily waiting to confront her but eventually, I talked myself out of it. Instead of facing the facts, I went into denial and made up excuses for her deceptions.

After I'd healed up and had gone back on duty, my partner and I received a disturbance call at a local motel. As we cruised through the parking lot, I saw her car parked in the back parking lot. As fate would have it, this motel was the one that my wife and her lover, a doctor who worked with her, had chosen for their rendezvous. Her car was parked alongside a big, black Mercedes that reeked of money. My partner, sensing I needed to deal with this alone, called for backup to handle the initial call while I made a call to her cell phone. It took a few rings but she finally answered, I made some small talk then I innocently asked her where she was. She lied and told me she was at work and she asked me how my shift was going. Through clenched teeth, I informed her that it just so happened that I was working a call at the Georgetown Hotel and I was parked in front of her car. Moments later, she came bursting out of one of the rooms hastily pulling on her clothes followed by a balding, pasty-faced creep in his boxers. A nasty confrontation in the parking lot between the three of us killed any feelings I had left for her especially when she screamed at me that she didn't love me anymore. We didn't talk again until the day we met in court to finalize the divorce. That day it was simply to say goodbye.

My thoughts were interrupted by Ryanne's phone ringing. "Hey!" she answered with a smile. I could tell who it was just from the look on her face and I felt the familiar twinge of jealousy.

"Yeah, Kimberly and I are headed to the set now. I have a one o'clock call time." She glanced at her watch and nodded. "I'm hoping I'll be able to watch some of it. I hate I can't be there with you. I love watching you race on that track."

She listened for a moment then said, "I love you too and be safe."

She hung up and I glanced in the mirror. "He's racing in Martinsville today, right?" I asked.

She nodded her head. "Yes, he drove up with the team yesterday and they'll be headed home tonight. Mason, I don't usually worry but for some reason, I feel weird about him racing today."

"He'll be fine," I assured her. "Those cars are full of features to keep him safe. He took me to the garage with him one day and showed me."

"I know. I'm being silly but I have a knot in my stomach. I'll be glad when the race is over and he calls," she said as she nervously bit her lip.

Her phone rang again and I saw her face light up again. "Hey, dude! Are you having a good day? Do you like the aquarium?" Her face grew serious. "I'm sorry the fish scared you! What a mean old fish!" She listened again then smiled. "Mason, Gage wants me to tell you he got you a seashell."

I grinned. "Cool!"

They talked for a few more minutes about the aquarium and as I pulled up in front of the location for the shoot, she said goodbye. "I love you, buddy. I'll see you when I get finished with work. Kisses!"

I parked the car and rushed around to help them get out. She and Kimberly headed for her trailer, and I quickly checked in with the set security officer Sam Bailey. Since the scene was being shot on location, they'd roped off the area, and Sam told me he'd already had a couple of fans asking if Ryanne was working. He gave me brief descriptions so I could keep an eye on things because only two weeks before, the actor Simon Piner had been cut by a zealous female fan who'd been upset by his recent engagement. Fans were getting bolder and bolder and both Rusty and Ryanne had a pretty big fan base. It was virtually impossible to predict when and where a threat could come from.

From behind me, I heard a man say, "Who's the big guy with the ponytail and earring?" Without turning around, I chuckled. I knew he was talking about me. Another voice I recognized as Bryan the producer informed him that I was Ryanne's security. He whistled and said under his breath, "That dude is massive!" Bryan laughed as they walked away no doubt making up some scary stories about me. A few minutes later, the call came for Ryanne to be on the set. I knocked on the trailer door and she emerged looking absolutely stunning. The movie was set during the Civil War and she was dressed in a period costume. The dress was off the shoulders with a big hoop skirt. A ribbon tied around her ample waist

13

accentuated her belly which was a crucial part of her character's condition. The costume designer had chosen the perfect shade of blue to complement her eyes, and her upswept blonde ringlets were held in place with a matching ribbon. She carried a parasol and had dainty white gloves on her hands. I held out my hand to help her down the step and she gave me a shy smile. Having worked with her on previous projects, I could tell she was already in character and I kept silent to keep it that way. I escorted her to the set, then stepped back to watch the magic happen. Her character was Victoria, a pregnant woman in the middle of the war trying to find her missing husband, Holt. I knew this because she'd rehearsed her lines as we'd traveled. Today's scene was really difficult for her because she was going to find out that her husband's body had just been brought in.

When George Poston the director called action, she began to spin in the street, calling out frantically to passersby, desperate for some help. Finally, a young soldier, seeing her distress, came to her aid. He led her down the street to the stately church in the center of town that was now being used as a makeshift hospital. When they reached the doorway, George called cut. It always amazed me how such a choppy shooting method could be edited together in the end to make a seamless movie. He walked over to Ryanne and complimented her on such a perfect take. The next one they were setting up was in the building where she would discover that her husband was one of the casualties. The makeup team came in to do some touchups while they checked the lighting. Ryanne took the opportunity to sit on a pew to get off of her feet and sip some water. It was an unusually hot day and I knew she had to be feeling uncomfortable in her heavy costume.

George called for the next scene so Ryanne made her way over to the door of the building to get to her mark. The cameras were set up inside so it would show her coming in the door, then follow her on a trolley as she made her way through the rows of the dead and wounded. Onlookers couldn't go inside so Kimberly and I stood where we could both see in the window. He called action once again and she slowly began to make her way through the building. The expression on her face was desperate, searching for her husband but also hoping he wasn't there.

Suddenly, her face contorted and she clutched her belly. Tears began to cascade down her cheeks as she cried, "No! No!" She dropped to her knees beside the actor who was portraying her husband. His head was wrapped in bloody bandages, his eyes lifeless. "Holt, you said you'd never leave me!" She cried as she buried her face in her hands. The pain on her face was so heart-wrenching that for a moment, I had to look away. I couldn't bear to see her so upset, so broken. She was definitely an amazing actress. George was watching mesmerized until he realized he needed to call cut. With an emotional voice, he did and everyone stood there silently watching Ryanne stand as she wiped the tears from her eyes. The crew slowly began to applaud and finally a smile came to her face. George walked over, took her in his arms and gave her a big hug. Everyone around me was buzzing about how beautiful the scene was. I was totally blown away and had a whole new level of respect for Ryanne and her craft.

"So, did I get big, bad Mason teary-eyed?" I turned to see Ryanne walking toward me with a big grin on her face.

I cleared my throat before answering. "Me? Nah. I've got a heart of steel. It would take more than that to break through it." Inside, I was a wreck. She had touched a part of my heart that I never knew existed. I was wrong to have these feelings for her and no matter what, I needed to keep them buried as deep as possible if I were going to continue to work with her.

Kimberly came up holding Ryanne's cell phone. "Hey, you just missed a call from Rusty. Also, do you mind if I get a ride back to the hotel with Brad? He asked me to dinner," she gushed.

"Brad? The cameraman?" When Kimberly blushed and nodded furiously, Ryanne laughed. "Well, of course...you deserve a break."

As soon as Kimberly dashed off, Ryanne called Rusty and he answered immediately. She had him on speakerphone so I could hear cheering in the background. "Hey, babe! How'd you do?" she asked excitedly.

"We won!" More cheering ensued.

"Yay! I knew you'd win!" she gushed. "What time are you heading home?"

"We're gonna wrap up some interviews then we'll be on our way."

"Okay, just be careful. Call me when you get there." Her face softened. "Babe, I love you."

"I love you too! See ya soon!"

She hung up and held out her phone to me. "Can you carry this, please? I don't have any pockets in this darn dress."

"Sure." I took it and slipped it into my pocket.

As we arrived at her trailer, she said, "Do you mind? I'm going to grab a quick shower then we can head back to the hotel. This hair is driving me nuts," she moaned as she yanked on a ringlet. To give her privacy, I waited on a chair outside until she was ready. She came out wearing baggy sweats and a loose fitting maternity top. Her damp hair hung down around her shoulders giving off the faintest scent of coconut as she walked past me.

We strolled to the car and found a few fans sitting on the sidewalk anxiously waiting for an autograph. They gushed about how beautiful she was and how pregnancy agreed with her. Despite her fatigue, she graciously signed the notebooks, posters, and pictures they held out to her and posed for photos. One of the ladies pointed at me and said, "Is he your bodyguard? He's hot!" Ryanne nodded and gave me a wink. I pretended not to hear and went about opening the door for her. After she'd signed the last autograph, she slid into the back seat and lay her head back with a sigh.

"I bet you're beat," I said over my shoulder as I climbed into the driver's seat.

She nodded and tried to stifle a yawn. "Yes, I really am. I never worked while I was pregnant with Gage. It takes a lot more energy."

We drove in silence to the hotel which was only a few miles away and when I glanced into the mirror, I could see she'd already fallen asleep. Her mouth was slightly open, her head rocking gently with the movement of the car. As I pulled up to the front of the hotel, the valet came running out to take the car so I quietly opened her door then gently shook her awake. Her eyes popped open and for a moment, she looked confused about where she was but then she focused on me and smiled. Holding out my hand, I helped her climb out and she leaned on me as we went up to her suite. At the door, she unlocked it then turned to give me a side hug. "Thank you so much, Mason," she said sleepily.

I patted her shoulder, trying to keep focused on anything but the urge to take her into my arms. My thoughts were anything but professional and I kicked myself for even thinking them. I knew in my heart that I should ask Ryder to assign me to another client but I couldn't imagine anyone else taking care of her like I would.

Her hands slid from around my waist and she looked up at me and smiled. "You have a good night and I'll call you if I need you." Reluctantly, I let her go and turned to go to my room which was right across the hall.

"Lock up and I'll check on you later," I said with a small wave. As I heard her door close, I whispered, "Goodnight." I unlocked my door and once inside, leaned against it until I heard it click. Standing there with my eyes closed, I imagined a different goodnight. In my mind, she'd look up at me with her deep blue eyes and I would slowly lean toward her until our mouths touched. Feeling her respond, my hands would wrap around her waist and her sweet lips would part ever so slightly. I'd softly stroke her tongue with mine until our breaths came in short bursts. Her fingertips would trail up my back, and then her nails would dig into my skin to urge me closer to her. I'd tangle my hands into her silky hair trapping her mouth against mine, never letting her go.

Suddenly, my phone rang jarring me back to reality. Glancing at it before I answered, I saw that it was Ryder was calling.

"What's up, Boss?"

"Mason, where's Ryanne?"

"She's in her room, why?"

I heard him take a deep breath. "Mason, there's been an accident. I have a friend who works with the highway patrol. He just called me because he knows we work security for her. He's trying desperately to get in touch with her."

I could barely speak. "Ryder, what's happened?"

He paused. "Man, it's Rusty. He was killed just about an hour ago when the truck they were riding in had a blow-out and lost control. It hit a guardrail and flipped into the path of an eighteen wheeler. Everyone in the pickup was killed."

I heard what he said, but it just didn't want to register. "He's dead? No, he can't be! Dude, he just talked to her!" I slumped to the floor since my legs no longer supported me.

"I know it's a shock. The driver and the front seat passenger were airlifted to the hospital but died on the way. Rusty was killed instantly."

I took a deep breath trying to collect myself. "Ryder, what can I do?"

Ryder's voice broke. "I don't know what to tell you. When the trooper gives her the bad news, she's going to need you more than ever. God, when I think about that little boy…"

Gage. The thought of that little boy losing his dad was like a knife in my gut. And the new baby would never know his or her father. Tears welled in my eyes but I fought them back. I needed to be strong for Ryanne. She was going to need every bit of support she could get.

"Mason, the trooper should be there any minute. I told him you'd meet him in the lobby. He'll fill you in on anything else you need to know. The media hasn't been alerted yet, thank God. We need to protect her from the news reports when the story does break. She's going to be bombarded with this and she's going to need you to get her through."

I nodded as I climbed from the floor. "I'll do my best. Thanks for calling me."

"Call me later with an update," Ryder said before he hung up.

In a daze, I took the elevator down to the lobby and within ten minutes, a highway patrol officer came through the doors. He saw me and came over with his hand extended.

"Sergeant Gordon," he said as he shook my hand.

23

"Mason Leffler. I'm Mrs. MacNeil's bodyguard."

He took off his hat and scrubbed his hand through his closely cropped hair. "This part of the job is the worst. I appreciate you being here for the family."

"Sir, I wouldn't have it any other way," I said as we boarded the elevator. "I don't know if you are aware but there are some special circumstances. Mrs. MacNeil is about eight months pregnant and she has a little boy named Gage."

"Damn," he said and he shifted his weight from side to side nervously. "That's tragic. I'll keep all that in mind. I appreciate you telling me."

The elevator came to a halt and the doors opened. We both hesitated for a moment, no doubt we were both feeling the same way. He finally stepped off and I followed. My legs felt like lead, my body moving in slow motion. We arrived at her door and with a brief hesitation, he knocked.

Chapter 2

Ryanne

My eyelids felt like lead and I kept hoping the knocking would stop but it wouldn't. With a groan, I crawled from the couch and looked at the clock. It was seven o'clock, it had to be Mrs. Jamison bringing Gage back from the aquarium.

"Did you forget your key again?" I asked as I peered out the peephole. Instead of Mrs. Jamison and my son, I saw Mason and a state trooper. My heart skipped a beat. Suddenly, I couldn't breathe. I slowly opened the door and waited for either of them to speak. "Please, dear God, tell me Gage is okay," I finally said as I searched Mason's face for a sign.

"Mrs. MacNeil, may I come in? I need to speak with you." Numbly, I backed into the room. The trooper took a deep breath. "Ma'am, I'm Sergeant Gordon. There's no easy way to say this. I regret to inform you that

25

your husband was killed in a motor vehicle accident this afternoon."

Blood rushed to my head and the room started spinning. Mason rushed to my side as I began to drop to the floor and he gently eased me onto a chair. Tears sprang to my eyes. "You must be mistaken. I talked to my husband. He's fine. He won the race."

Sergeant Gordon shook his head. "I'm so sorry. It's not a mistake. He was traveling with two of his teammates when the truck they were riding in lost control and…"

Mason interrupted him. "Perhaps we can leave the details until later when she can process them."

He nodded. "Certainly. Ma'am, I'm sorry for your loss. We are at your disposal, if you need anything."

Suddenly it hit me. "Gage, oh my God. What am I going to tell Gage?" I cried as I gripped Mason's arm tightly. "Mason, what am I going to do?"

Mason held me tightly letting me sob against his shoulder. My hand absently stroked my belly and I felt the baby kick against it. My child, who now had lost a father before they ever got to know him. The pain was piercing, like a knife in my heart. I still couldn't catch my breath, and I started to panic and become dizzy. Mason captured my face in his hands and forced me to look into his eyes. "Ryanne, you have to slow your breathing down. You're going to hyperventilate and that's not good for you or the baby."

I was caught in a whirlpool that was pulling me down but as I focused on Mason's voice, it began to slow. My children needed me and no matter what, I had to be strong for them.

Sergeant Gordon squatted down in front of me. "Mrs. MacNeil, we're prepared to escort you back to Charlotte whenever you're able." My mind was spinning and my thoughts jumbled. We'd just spoken on the phone! How could this happen?

Mason gently dabbed my eyes with a tissue. "Ryanne, Gage will be here any minute. Do you want to go into the bathroom and splash some water on your face? Can I get you anything?"

Shaking my head no, I rose unsteadily to my feet and made my way to the bathroom. Once inside, I shut the door, sat on the edge of the tub, and buried my face in a towel to muffle my sobs. Finally, after several minutes, they subsided and I was able to walk to the vanity where I turned on the cold water. I looked up and the reflection I saw in the mirror was a stranger. Red-rimmed, swollen eyes reflected back at me. I quickly splashed the cold water onto my flaming cheeks. The cold shocked me but it also felt good, like a slap in the face, bringing me back to reality. I needed to get myself together because the person I saw in the mirror would scare the hell out of Gage. I dried off my face, ran a brush through my hair and with a deep, shuddering breath opened the door.

Gage had indeed come home and I found him sitting on Mason's knee staring at the trooper with a look of awe. When he saw me, his face lit up. "Momma!" He didn't act as if anything were unusual so I breathed a sigh of relief for that. I walked over to him and ran my fingers through his hair.

"Hey, baby." He scrambled from Mason's lap and wrapped his arms tightly around my hips. Mrs. Jamison was standing next to Sergeant Gordon and I could tell she had heard the news. As evenly as possible, I asked, "Can you get him packed?"

She nodded then hugged me tightly. "Whatever you need, I'm here for you," she whispered in my ear.

I nodded giving her a half smile. "Thank you. I'm going to need all the help I can get."

She led Gage by the hand to the bedroom and shut the door. Another wave of emotion rolled through me and I began to sway. Mason wrapped me in a hug to steady me. "Ryanne, I'm worried about you. You should have something to drink. Have a seat, I'll get it for you." I dropped onto the edge of the couch and he returned moments later with a glass of water. I eagerly gulped some down feeling the cold rush into my body. "You're getting some color back now," he said taking the glass from my shaking hand.

"This is a bad dream, isn't it?" I asked hopefully.

He shook his head. "No, I'm sorry to say, it's real."

"Has the media found out? I don't want Rusty's parents to see it on the news. I need to call them."

"The highway patrol has kept it out of the news so far but I agree, you'll need to tell them as soon as possible."

I looked around the room for my phone but couldn't find it. "Mason, can you find my phone?"

Mason reached into his pocket. "I've got it. You gave it to me earlier."

My phone battery was dead and I suddenly remembered that the battery was low when I gave it to him. He quickly found the charger and plugged it in. After it charged enough to use it, I began to search the contacts for his parent's number when suddenly a voicemail chimed. I looked up at Mason. "Oh, God. What if it was Rusty?" I whispered.

"Do you need me to listen to it?" he asked holding out his hand for the phone.

I took a deep breath and shook my head no. "I think I can do this." I pressed the button to listen and then I heard the last call my husband would ever make.

"Hey, beautiful! We stopped to get some gas so I thought I'd call while the guys are in the store. I just wanted to say, I love you and give my babies kisses from their daddy tonight. I really miss you. Come home soon, the bed's gonna be just too empty without you. Talk to you when I get home, okay? Bye, baby." The voicemail ended and the phone dropped from my hand into my lap. I felt a weird tingling in my mouth, and then the world went dark.

"I think she's starting to come around," I heard someone say as I struggled to open my eyes. "Ryanne, can you hear me?"

I was so confused. What had happened? Everything seems so fuzzy and weird. I opened my eyes and see Mason kneeling beside the couch where I was now laying. He looked so worried and it scared me and then I saw the trooper. My heart began racing as everything that had happened came rushing back like a tidal wave. "Oh, God. He's gone, isn't he?" I cried.

Mason's fingers tightened around mine. "I'm afraid so."

"Where's Gage?" I couldn't hide the panic in my voice.

"He's napping in the bedroom. He was so exhausted from the aquarium that he ran out of steam. Mrs. Jamison is keeping an eye on him."

"Let me check her blood pressure again," a man standing next to Mason said.

"Ryanne, this is Dr. Averitt. We called him when you passed out. He's been monitoring you and the baby."

I allowed the doctor to place the cuff around my arm and just lay there silently, my hand resting on my belly, tears silently streaming from my eyes. "Everything looks good," he said finally. "I would feel better if you were hospitalized for observation."

I shook my head no. "I can't leave Gage."

Dr. Averitt nodded. "Okay, but I would suggest you remain here at least until the morning. You need to rest."

Sergeant Gordon and Mason were both nodding in agreement so I said, "Fine, I'll rest until morning. I do need to make some phone calls though."

Mason brought my phone to me and I placed the call to Rusty's parents that I never wanted to have to make. Many tears later, I hung up exhausted. His mom and dad were devastated but also deeply concerned for my own well-being. I assured them that I was in good hands and that the baby was fine. I called my own parents next and, of course, they wanted to come right away. After explaining that I wasn't home, I promised that I'd let them know when I got back so they could arrange to fly in from Phoenix.

The doctor wanted to give me a mild sedative to help me rest but I didn't want it. I needed to keep my head straight and figure out what to do next. He left me a prescription that was safe to take, along with orders to call him if I needed anything.

Sergeant Gordon arranged to escort us back to Charlotte the next morning and it was then I remembered I hadn't finished filming yet. "Mason, what about the movie?"

He rested his hand on my shoulder. "All taken care of. The director said he has all the scenes he needs from you and he sends his condolences."

I sighed and leaned my head back against the pillow. My head was throbbing as if it were going to explode. It actually hurt to think. I tried to relax but my thoughts kept going back to Rusty. Finally, exhaustion took hold, my eyelids grew heavy, and I fell into a deep sleep.

Chapter 3

Mason

I sat in the chair across from her bed and watched her sleep. I didn't want to leave in case she woke up and needed something. Her eyelids fluttered as she dreamt, her breath coming in short bursts. Suddenly, she sat straight up and cried out, "NO!"

I rushed to her side. "You're okay." I sat on the edge of the bed and pulled her into my arms. She sagged against me, sobs racking her body.

"M-Mason…what am I going to do?" She cried.

I grabbed some tissues and dabbed her cheeks. "I don't know…I just don't know."

Her crying subsided and she lay back in the bed. I pulled the sheet up and tucked her in. "Try to get some sleep. I'm right here if you need me."

She kept a grip on my arm so I eased myself back on to the edge of the bed. I tucked her into the crook of my arm and she rested her head on my shoulder. "Thank you for being here," she whispered.

She soon fell back to sleep and I watched over her, my own eyes heavy but never closing. A few hours later, the sun started to creep up as the dawn began to break. My arm was numb but I didn't care. She needed sleep as evidenced by the dark circles under her eyes. Finally, she began to stir. She opened her eyes and looked up at me. "Hey," she said softly.

"How are you feeling?" I asked and helped her sit up.

She yawned and stretched. "The headache from hell is easing off but I still feel like crap. How's Gage?"

"He woke up a little while ago and wanted to come in here to check on you. He's worried."

She buried her face in her hands. "I don't know how I'm going to tell him. I can't, I just can't."

"Well, the media found out somehow and the story hit the news about an hour ago. It's everywhere." Her eyes immediately filled with tears.

"Can you get Gage for me?" She wiped her eyes and ran her fingers through her hair. I went to the bedroom and called for him. He came running in but stopped when he saw his mom. He jumped up into the bed beside her and wrapped his tiny arms around her. I closed the door and left them alone.

A little while later, Ryanne and Gage came out of the bedroom. He was holding her hand tightly and chattering away about a big fish he saw at the aquarium. Mrs. Jamison took him by the hand. "Can you get him ready to leave? It's time we head home." She nodded sadly and led Gage to the bedroom.

"So how did it go?" I asked.

"I can't expect him to fully understand what happened but he did ask questions and I tried my best to answer them." She sighed. "Mason, what's the plan for getting out of here? I don't want to face any press." She absently rubbed her lower back.

"Well, I've arranged for us to leave by the back door. Hopefully, no one has been tipped off that we're going out that way." A few minutes later, the bellhop came to the door and carefully loaded their things onto the luggage cart.

Sergeant Gordon arrived shortly after with two additional officers. "Mrs. MacNeil, we're ready to escort you when you're ready."

Ryanne nodded sadly. "I can't hide from this anymore, let's go."

When Mrs. Jamison came out of the room with Gage, I picked him up and held him in my arms. My reasoning was that it was safer for him to be out of any potential rush of people and my goal was to get him into the vehicle as soon as possible. Ryanne stayed right by my side, her hand resting protectively on Gage's leg. The officers led the way down the hallway and to the waiting elevator. Our ride down was eerily silent but as soon as the doors opened, I immediately saw that our planned escape had been leaked to the press. The blaze of camera flashes was blinding but I kept my focus on our car which was parked at the curb. We pushed our way through the crowd and I could hear people shouting as we passed.

"We love you, Ryanne!"

"We love Rusty!"

Ryanne kept her composure but I could tell the outpouring of support from the fans was overwhelming her. The ladies bundled into the car where Kimberly was already waiting and after making sure everyone was secure, we pulled away behind the lead trooper car. We left Wilmington and began our long journey to Charlotte.

The trip was quiet, Gage slept and the ladies talked quietly among themselves. When we stopped at a rest area for a stretch, I overheard Ryanne talking to Ryder. "I want you to assign someone to stay at my house round the clock when I get home. I'd feel better knowing that Gage and I are safe."

As she hung up, she noticed me watching her. "Mason, I'm sorry but I don't expect you to be with us all day every day. You've been with me all through the Wilmington shoot, I just figured you'd be sick of us by now."

"If you don't want me, then I'll step away," I said as evenly as possible.

She shook her head vehemently. "No, that's not what I meant. I just didn't want to make you feel like you *had* to be there. If you want us, we're yours."

I nodded slowly. "Yes, I want to be there for you."

"Fine," she said placing another call. "Ryder, it's Ryanne again. Never mind about the security. Mason's going to do it." She hung up and studied me for a moment. "You'll let me know if you change your mind?"

"Yes, I'll let you know."

"Okay, then I guess we've got an understanding," she said sliding back into the car.

Several hours later when we arrived at the gate to the house, there were flower arrangements and wreaths piled up against the fence. A group of fans were milling around at the edge of the property, kept at bay by the local police. When they saw our car, they began waving and shouting words of support to Ryanne. Glancing in the mirror, I saw her wipe her eyes as she took in it all in.

Once inside the house, Ryanne was met by Thomas Aldean the owner of Rusty's race team. They went into the study and shut the door for privacy so in the meantime, I helped unload their things from the car. About an hour later, they emerged and I could tell they'd both been crying.

"Mason," Ryanne said beckoning me to the staircase. "You'll need to put your things somewhere. Let's get you a bedroom."

We got to the top of the stairs. She pointed out her bedroom and then Gage's. On the opposite side of the house, there were four massive bedrooms, each with their own en suite bathroom. I chose the one with the closest proximity to their rooms in case of emergency and set my things down on the bed. "This will be fine," I said looking around the tastefully decorated room. The king-sized cherry wood bed was covered in a deep burgundy silk coverlet accented by at least a dozen throw pillows. There was a sitting area consisting of an oversized arm chair overlooking the six-foot window.

"I hope you'll be comfortable," Ryanne said softly.

41

Nodding, I said, "Thank you."

She turned on her heel and went to the door. "If you need anything, just ask. I think I'm going to lay down for a while."

I unpacked my things reminding myself to stop by my apartment the next time I was in town to get some more clothes. I turned on the television and was bombarded by the news of Rusty's untimely death.

The news channel had a reporter stationed outside the gate at the house. "Good evening. Tonight the racing world is still reeling from the news that popular driver Rusty MacNeil was killed in an automobile accident yesterday evening. His widow, Ryanne Charles, has just returned to their home on Lake Norman and was greeted by hundreds of fans and flower arrangements."

The camera panned away from the reporter to show the piles of flowers and cards. Interspersed with the flowers were teddy bears, no doubt for Gage. The reporter walked over to some fans standing nearby.

"Excuse me," he said turning to an older woman holding a sign that read *Rusty will always be my #1!* "I understand you have been out here ever since the news broke. What did Rusty MacNeil mean to you?"

The woman wiped her eyes with a well-used tissue. "He was so handsome and funny and a hell of a race car driver. He was a nice guy and never wrecked anybody. I don't know if I can watch racing anymore."

The reporter patted her on the shoulder as she broke down in tears. He quickly turned to a man standing nearby, dressed from head to toe in Rusty's team apparel. "Sir, what does this mean for racing?"

The man cleared his throat, obviously emotional. "I knew Rusty when he was a boy. He'd race anything with wheels. His daddy and I were in business together and we were his first sponsors. I can't believe this happened and my thoughts and prayers go out to Ryanne and Gage."

The reporter nodded then turned to the camera. "No doubt the next few days will be tremendously difficult for Rusty's family. Sources tell us in addition to a private family service that a public memorial is being considered. We'll keep you updated with the details as soon as we get word."

I shut the television off and decided to go down and walk the fence of the property to make sure there weren't any areas that were likely to be breached. The police were still stationed at the gate keeping the fans orderly as they filed by to drop off their remembrances.

I walked down to the shoreline of the lake and saw the police had already considered someone might try to get to the property via the water. They had a boat stationed just off the shore, prepared to intercept anyone who might want to try to get too close to Ryanne.

I went back into the house and up to my room. I grabbed a shower then turned on the television, being sure to leave the news channels alone. I found a comedy show and lay on the bed to watch. The lack of sleep from the night before caught up with me and I promptly fell asleep.

A siren on the television woke me up and glancing at the clock, I saw it was after midnight. My stomach growled and I realized I'd never eaten dinner. Making my way through the dark quiet house, I found the kitchen and after rummaging through the cupboards, found some peanut butter and jelly. I whipped up a couple of sandwiches and poured myself a glass of milk then decided to go out onto the porch to get some fresh air.

As I stepped onto the porch, I heard a trembling voice say, "What am I going to do?" I stopped in my tracks and listened. "You weren't supposed to leave me." Ryanne was gently swinging on the large porch swing with her head laid back and her eyes closed.

I felt awkward about intruding into her space so I took a step back and found what had to be the creakiest board on the porch. At the sound, she lifted her head and her eyes popped open to focus on me. "Mason…"

I took another step back. "I'm sorry. I didn't know anyone was out here."

"Please, don't leave. I was just sitting here talking to myself."

I walked over to a rocking chair, set my food and milk on the small table and sat down. "Would you like a sandwich?" I asked holding the plate out to her.

"No, thank you. I managed to eat some soup earlier but the thought of food makes me kind of nauseous right now. My nerves are shot."

I nodded silently and took a bite of the sandwich. She closed her eyes and rocked slowly back and forth. The night was filled with sounds of crickets and frogs and the sky was filled with stars.

I was startled when she spoke. "Mason, have you ever been married?"

I hesitated choosing my words carefully. Now wasn't the time for ex-bashing. I could tell she needed to talk to someone who knew what it felt like to have what she had.

"Yes." I took a sip of my milk giving her a chance to take the lead. When I glanced her way, she was looking at me intently.

"Did you love her?" Her eyes were glistening with unshed tears.

"I did. I guess a part of me always will."

She absently tucked her hair behind her ear. "Do you mind telling me what happened?" When I didn't answer right away, she started to stand. "I'm sorry. I'm getting into your business."

"No, it's okay. Please, sit." She eased back onto the swing. "She and I had different opinions on having kids."

"So, you didn't want them?" she asked.

I chuckled. "Everyone assumes that. No, I was the one who wanted them. At first, she said she wanted a big family. After we got married, she got a great job and that became her sole focus. She was so into her career, kids became the last thing on her mind."

She placed her hand on her belly. "Rusty and I always knew we wanted kids. I got pregnant so easily with Gage that when we decided it was time for another, we thought it would be a piece of cake." She shook her head and laughed softly. "That wasn't how it worked out. When I didn't get pregnant right away, we went to the doctor to get tested. It turned out I was the problem. Rusty was so sweet. He told me that it didn't matter and that Gage was all we needed. With the pressure off, a few months later, I found out I was pregnant with this baby."

"And you didn't want to know what you're having?" I asked as I began to rock in my chair.

She shook her head. "The answer to that question is written down in an envelope." Suddenly, she covered her face with her hands. "Oh, God. Rusty will never know." She began to cry so I got up and joined her on the swing.

"Ryanne, I believe he already knows."

"Do…do you think so?" She sniffled and rested her head on my shoulder.

"I do. Now, let's get you upstairs so you can rest. You have a long day ahead." I helped her get off the swing and led her into the house. As we got to her bedroom door, I squeezed her arm lightly. "Goodnight."

She turned to go into her room then she stopped. "Thank you for listening, Mason. And in my opinion, after seeing you with Gage, I know you'd have made a great dad." She gave me a sad smile then closed the door behind her.

Chapter 4

Ryanne

The next few days went by in a blur. Rusty's parents arrived along with my own. They were invaluable while I was making the funeral arrangements. We planned a private service at the MacNeil family cemetery and then, with the help of the racing community, planned a public memorial in one of the largest churches in Charlotte. I wanted the race fans to be able to say goodbye and from the tributes left at my gate, many wanted to attend.

I was sitting on the big leather couch by myself in the conservatory looking out the window when I heard a knock at the door. "Come in," I called.

The door opened and Mason stuck his head in. "Ryanne, I'm sorry to bother you but one of the troopers just dropped off Rusty's personal effects."

My heart began to beat faster. The thought of seeing his things scared me but I knew this was part of the process. "Could you bring them in, please?"

He brought a large manila envelope to me which I took with trembling hands. "Thank you." He turned to leave but I stopped him. "Please stay here with me while I open this, if you don't mind."

"I don't mind," he said as he sat in the chair next to me.

Breaking the seal on the envelope, I let the contents slip out onto my lap. The first thing that caught my eye was Rusty's wedding band. It was a simple gold band engraved on the inside with the date of our wedding. I unhooked the chain from around my neck and slipped it on before clasping it back again. His phone and wallet were there as well. I saw something unusual sticking out of his wallet. It was a white envelope. As I unfolded it, I saw what it was and I literally lost my breath. On the outside, it read, *Baby MacNeil.*

"Oh, my God. He had this with him," I said, my voice breaking. I handed the envelope to Mason. "I didn't want to find out then but I think I need to know now. Will you open it and read it to me?"

Mason opened the envelope and slipped the piece of paper out. He studied it for a moment and then said with a sad smile, "It's a girl."

I lay my head back against the couch and sighed. "A girl," I whispered. "As pretty as her mama."

Mason cleared his throat. "Ryanne, there's something else."

My eyes popped open. "What is it?"

He held the paper out to me and that was when I saw Rusty's handwriting. Pulling it to me, through tear-filled eyes, I read, *"I knew it! Sorry, I couldn't wait...Love you! Rusty xx."*

Suddenly, I started laughing through my tears. Mason was smiling as well. "How does that make you feel?" he asked.

I pictured Rusty sneaking a peek at that paper and it made me happy that he knew we were having a girl. "I should have known he'd look," I said folding the note then slipping it back into the envelope. "He's so impatient about everything."

Mason nodded. "I hope this brings you some peace of mind." He stood and gently squeezed my shoulder. "I'll be outside if you need anything."

He walked to the door then he turned. "He was a very lucky man." He left shutting the door quietly behind him.

The next morning was the private memorial service. We decided to keep it simple with only immediate family attending. The public memorial would be where all of his friends and fans could gather and pay tribute to his life. I went through the motions at the service but at the end of the day, I couldn't remember much of anything that happened. The one thing that stayed with me was how much I was going to miss him and how tragic this was for our children.

Later that night, I sat on the staircase listening to the conversations drifting up. My parents were talking with Rusty's and in the midst of them all was Gage.

He had no idea what was going on, only that his daddy wasn't going to be coming home. When he'd asked where he was, I said the first thing I could think of, "He's living in the sky with God." That was when he decided he wanted to send his daddy some balloons to make him happy.

"He's an amazing kid."

I looked around to see Mason coming down the stairs.

"Yeah, I think he's the only thing holding me together."

Mason sat down on the step beside me. "When I was a cop, I saw so many horrible things, the worst was domestic violence. Families would be torn apart and in the middle of it all would be a small child caught in the crossfire. It broke my heart to see them headed to foster care because they had to be taken from their home. I kept a stash of stuffed toys in my trunk for those situations and when I handed a little boy or girl something they could hold on to, their face would always brighten up."

I totally understood what he meant. You couldn't possibly expect a child to understand a loss, especially at his age. The best thing I could do as his mother was keep the memory of his father alive.

My dad came into the foyer and saw us sitting on the steps. "You okay?" he asked me, concern on his face.

"Yeah, Dad. I'm just tired. I'm going to go to bed. We have a busy day tomorrow." He nodded and went back into the den where, from the sound of things, Gage still commanding their attention.

As I started to get up, I felt Mason take me by the arm. "Here, let me help you."

"Lord, I don't want you to hurt yourself. I feel like a whale," I moaned.

He laughed. "You've got to be kidding! You're one of the most beautiful pregnant ladies I've ever known."

"Bless your heart, you *are* sweet but I know how I look and feel."

He shook his head. "I stand by my assessment."

Holding my elbow to steady me, he led me up the stairs to my room. "Thanks again, Mason. I'll see you in the morning."

I went into my room and closed the door then dropped onto the bed exhausted. My body was worn out but my mind wouldn't stop. All I could think about was facing another day without Rusty. I climbed into our king-sized bed and curled up into a tight ball as the tears began to flow again.

The next morning, I felt Gage leap onto my bed. He crawled up beside me and snuggled himself under my arm. I rolled over and turned on the television to find some cartoons which we watched quietly until I realized if we didn't get up, I'd be late. I decided not to let Gage attend either the funeral or the memorial service, instead choosing to have our own private time with just the two of us after everything was over.

I walked Gage to his room and helped him get dressed. Mrs. Jamison had two grandchildren his age and they were going to spend the day playing together at the house. After giving him a kiss, I went back to my own room to try to get myself ready. With a lot of effort, I managed to dress and I pulled my hair into a ponytail because I just didn't feel up to doing my hair. A knock at my door startled me.

"Ryanne, it's time," Mason said softly. Taking a deep breath, I slipped on my shoes and opened the door. Mason gave me a sad smile. "You look lovely."

"Thank you," I whispered. He offered his arm and I grasped him tightly needing his strength. We met the family at the bottom of the stairs where my dad was waiting to escort me to the limo. Mason made sure we were all safely inside then joined the driver in the front seat. We drove in silence out of the gates and I was overwhelmed once again by the enormous outpouring of love and support by the fans who were standing there waving as we passed. Along the way, we passed signs honoring Rusty. As we pulled up to the front of the church, Mason turned to us.

"We have a team waiting to escort you into the service. I'll signal when we're ready for you to exit the car."

My dad turned to me. "Are you feeling okay? You look really pale."

Trying to still my trembling hands, I nodded. "Yes, I'll be okay." I stepped from the car and as we approached the doors of the church, the world suddenly went black.

Faintly, I could hear someone calling my name. "Ryanne, are you okay? She's not responding, call 911." I fought through the haze and managed to open my eyes slightly. I could see several people hovering over me and it confused me. What had happened? Where was I? I tried to move but then realized I was being held in someone's arms. "I'm getting her back to the car. We can get to a hospital quicker that way." It was Mason's voice. My head was clearing slowly and it all came rushing back to me. We were at Rusty's service.

"Mason," I managed to whisper. He stopped and looked at me.

"Oh, thank God." He sighed. He turned to my father who was rushing to open the door of the car. "She's coming around." He gently placed me on the seat of the car and I leaned back. Kneeling in front of me, he took my hand and said, "You passed out. I think it's best if we take you to the hospital to get you checked out."

Someone produced a bottle of water which he handed to me. I took a long drink, feeling the cold rush through me. "I think I'll be okay," I said softly. "I haven't eaten much lately and I think it caught up with me."

Mason's brows were creased with worry. "I think you need to be seen by a doctor. You have the baby to consider, as well."

I nodded. "I know, but I need to do this. I'm feeling better and I promise, after the service, I'll go."

He studied my face for a moment then nodded. "Okay." He held his hand out and I gripped it tightly. Leaning on both my dad and Mason, I entered the church. They led me to the front pew where I was seated next to my frantic mother and in-laws. They'd already been seated when they heard of a commotion outside and had been unsure of what to do. My mother held on to me tightly, with obvious concern on her face.

The service was beautiful, filled with music, tributes and a video montage of Rusty's racing career from when he'd started as a teenager to his final race – the one I'd missed in Martinsville. He was smiling and waving at the camera and through my tears, I smiled back. Mr. Aldean gave a beautiful eulogy which was full of wonderful memories. He spoke of how proud Rusty was of Gage and that he hoped one day that he would follow in his daddy's footsteps and be a driver. The service concluded with one of his best friends, Lucas Bryant, singing, "How Great Thou Art" and there wasn't a dry eye in the church. I was escorted to the waiting car in lieu of having a reception. It had been decided that it was going to be too much to have everyone offer their condolences to me so instead, the directors of the service invited them to write a note in a book that would be given to me later.

Once in the car, I lay my throbbing head back against the seat and closed my eyes. My parents were riding with me and my dad kept talking quietly to Mason. I only caught snatches of their conversation but it was mostly concern for my health and getting me seen by the doctor. A few minutes later, the car stopped. I opened my eyes to find we were in a parking garage.

"Ryanne, we're at your doctor's office. We're using the back door because we were followed by the press," Mason said as he opened the door.

I groaned. "Can't they leave me alone?"

He shook his head solemnly. "I'm afraid not."

We rode in the elevator to my doctor's office and were greeted by the receptionist. "Dr. Han is expecting you," she said. My mom took my hand and we followed her to the exam room. My dad and Mason stayed in the waiting area.

Dr. Han came in right away and checked my vitals. "Ryanne, I've been told you're not eating or sleeping much. I can give you something mild to help you rest but you must eat to ensure your baby is healthy."

I nodded as a single tear rolled down my cheek. "I know. It's just so hard."

"I understand completely." He patted my shoulder then made some notes in my chart. "I'm giving you a prescription to help you sleep. Call me tomorrow and let me know how it works for you."

I took the prescription and my mother and I joined my dad at the checkout desk. "Where's Mason?" I asked looking around.

My dad smiled. "He's checking out the perimeter." I could tell my dad appreciated Mason being there to protect Gage and myself. The last few days had been really stressful and knowing he was there was a huge comfort to me as well.

Mason came into the room, his eyes scanning the entire time. He gestured for us to follow and we rode back down to the waiting car. As we were climbing in, I heard someone shout, "Ryanne, how are you holding up?" followed by the flashes of cameras held right by the door. Mason shielded me with his body allowing me to get in without them getting a clear shot. There were groans of disappointment from the paparazzi as the door closed and we drove away.

Luckily, we were able to get away without them following us and we made it home safely. I felt as if the day had been a dream but the aches and pains of my pregnancy were also a major reality check. The doctor was right. I did need to take care of myself and my little girl.

I really hadn't thought much about the baby, as horrible as that may seem. I'd been so consumed with my own grief that I'd blocked it from my mind but as I lay in the dark on my bed, I felt her move as if to give me a wakeup call. I needed to be strong for Gage. I needed to be strong for –. It hit me that she didn't have a name. Rusty and I would have been picking a name together but now I was facing the task alone. I closed my eyes and whispered, "Help me," but I heard only silence. Burying my face in my pillow, I cried myself to sleep, knowing I was truly alone.

Chapter 5

Mason

I could hear muffled crying not long after she went into her room. I'd been coming up the stairs after checking to make sure everything was secure for the night when I'd heard her. I crept to her door and could hear her sobbing and it ripped my heart apart. Part of me wanted to comfort her but another part said no. She was a client and my responsibility, nothing else. I wished I could take her in my arms and hold her. She was so broken yet trying to hold herself together. The pain in her eyes was so raw yet she managed to show compassion for those who needed to share their grief with her. Truthfully, I was envious of the love she had for her husband but also I felt ashamed for feeling that way. The man was gone. He hadn't cheated. He hadn't run off. He'd died. Their love was still pure, not tainted by scandal and the memories she held would be cherished, not easily forgotten. Being with her, however, was making it harder for me to conceal my feelings. My heart would beat just a little faster when she called my name and I looked forward to seeing her every chance I could get. I knew that one day I'd end up having to leave her to keep my feelings from her. I couldn't bear the thought of that so I buried the feelings as deeply as I could hoping that she'd never see.

A week later, her parents and in-laws began packing up to leave to head back to their homes. I could see it was stressing Ryanne that they were leaving but they all had obligations back home to take care of. She assured them she was fine as she waved goodbye when the cars came to take them to the airport. Her mother had assured her that she'd be back in a few weeks to help when the baby was due. I watched as Gage clung to her leg as he had done a lot for the last several days.

Ryanne stayed home for the next several days and, with Kimberly's help, wrote thank you cards for the hundreds of flower arrangements that had been sent for Rusty's memorial. Otherwise, she kept to herself and I respected her space, keeping my distance but ready in case she needed me.

One morning, I was coming downstairs when I heard laughter coming from the kitchen. I walked in and found Ryanne and Gage sitting at the table having breakfast. Gage was trying to toss cereal into his mouth. Ryanne was showing him how to do it and I stood silently watching them realizing this was the first time I'd seen them like this in a while. Eventually, Ryanne noticed me standing at the door and she smiled. "Come in! Join us."

As I walked closer, the crunch of cereal under my shoes was evidence that Gage wasn't very good at catching his cereal. Glancing down, I shook my head and laughed. "Dude, you're going to need to practice."

He just smiled and held out a piece of cereal to me. I hesitated for a moment then took it. I readied myself, mouth open and flipped the cereal up in the air. Unfortunately, it landed on top of my head. Gage dissolved into a giggling fit and I looked over to find Ryanne hiding her laughter behind her hand. "Good try," she said with a snicker.

Shaking my head, I walked to the coffee pot to pour myself a cup. "I guess I'll have to practice too," I drawled.

She cocked her head to the side and smiled. "I guess you will."

I looked around the kitchen and noticed that Mrs. Jamison's things weren't on the counter as usual. Ryanne took a sip of her coffee and said, "Mrs. Jamison has the morning off. Today is going to be for some Mommy/Gage time."

I nodded slowly. This was a good sign. This just might be what she needed to get herself back on track. "So she'll be back this afternoon?" I asked as I sipped my coffee.

She smiled but her eyes only reflected sadness. "Yes, and of course, my mom will be coming back when the baby arrives to help as well." She stood up, holding her hand to her lower back. "Mason, will you take us to the park today? Gage wants to send some balloons to his daddy."

"Sure, just let me know when you're ready." I rinsed out my cup and headed out to pull the car around.

About thirty minutes later, Ryanne found me waiting in front of the house. She was holding Gage by his little hand and they quickly got settled into the truck. Gage was clapping his hands with excitement as we drove to the party store to get some balloons. Despite her objections, I went inside to get them, returning with a dozen bright blue ones. Gage giggled as I stuffed them into the back of the truck all around him. Ryanne had to laugh as well since they were surrounding her head taking up most of the back of the car. "Did you have to get a dozen?" She laughed. "One would have been fine."

"I had to get a dozen. Gage told me that's what he wanted."

She turned to Gage, who was happily punching at a stray balloon that peeked from behind his car seat. Looking back at me, she mouthed, *Thank you.*

With a nod, I drove them to the park. Once we'd unloaded the balloons, I handed the bouquet to Gage making sure to tie the strings to the strap of his overalls so it wouldn't blow away before they were ready. "I'll wait here," I said, prepared to watch from beside the car.

Gage took me by the hand and tugged. "Come," he grunted as he pulled on my hand. "Come with me."

Ryanne smiled as she shrugged her shoulders. "Looks like you have to come."

I let Gage lead me to a field in the park where there were just a few trees. He held the balloons as I untied the strings from his strap. Ryanne held his other hand and as she nodded to Gage, he let them go. His tiny voice said, "I love you, Daddy" as he watched them float slowly up into the sky then it was as if a strong wind lifted them up faster and higher. They grew smaller and smaller until they disappeared out of sight.

Ryanne took a deep breath then turned toward the truck. "Let's go, baby." Still holding Gage's hand, she slowly walked back. Gage wouldn't let go of my hand so we ended up walking together with him between us. She was discreetly wiping her eyes, no doubt trying to keep Gage from seeing her tears.

Back at the house, Mrs. Jamison was just getting out of her car when we pulled up. She took Gage, who was excitedly telling her about the balloons, upstairs to put him down for his nap. Ryanne went in to the den to lay down on the couch and I went into the kitchen to make myself a sandwich. I decided to make one for Ryanne in case she was hungry. When I came in to the room, I found her watching the video that had been played at the memorial. I didn't say a word, just sat down next to her. She turned to me and said with a sigh, "You must think I'm crazy. I can't stop watching this. It makes me feel as if he's still here."

Handing her the sandwich, I said, "You're not crazy. Everyone grieves differently and if it helps you at all, then it's a good thing."

She stopped the video then rested her hand on my arm. "Mason, I know you're supposed to be here to keep Gage and me safe, but I really consider you to be a friend. You've been so kind and supportive and I just felt that I needed to say that."

My chest constricted as I tried to keep my emotions in check. After taking a deep breath, I managed to look into her eyes, which were brimming with tears. "Ryanne…I appreciate that. I really do. You both mean a lot to me."

Suddenly, her face contorted and she moaned.

"Ryanne?"

Her face drained of color and she grabbed at her stomach. "Mason, oh God, I think my water just broke."

Confused, I did a quick calculation in my head. "But you aren't due for another few weeks."

"You're right, I'm not," she groaned. "This is not good."

"I'll call 911," I said reaching for my phone.

She grabbed my arm. "Tell them to make it fast."

I was able to get across the urgency to the 911 operator and by the time the EMTs arrived, Ryanne was having contractions only minutes apart. I ran upstairs to let Mrs. Jamison know what was going on as they got her onto the gurney and then I called Ryder, who said he'd come over to the house to make sure Gage was secure. I dashed downstairs in time to jump into the ambulance and with the siren wailing, we headed toward the hospital.

Holding my hand tightly, Ryanne had a light sheen of perspiration on her forehead and her hands were knotted into the thin sheet covering her. Her eyes met mine and I

71

gave her a reassuring smile which I could see helped calm her down. Once inside the ER, they rolled her straight through to the elevator. Keeping pace with the gurney, I managed to ask if she wanted me to call anyone to be with her.

She looked at me intently. "Please stay with me," she groaned. Nodding, I took her hand, giving it a gentle squeeze.

When we reached the Labor and Delivery floor, they wheeled her into a room where they transferred her to a bed. Nurses began to hook her up to monitors and I stepped back to allow them access. A doctor came in to do an exam so I stepped outside to give them some privacy. A moment later, a nurse came out. "Sir, your wife is asking for you."

Shaking my head, I said, "She's not my wife, I'm her bodyguard."

With obvious surprise, she said, "Well, she's asking for you."

I slowly opened the door to find Ryanne holding out her hand to me. "Mason, you said you'd stay with me."

I walked over to take her hand. The doctor looked up as I joined her. "Mr. Leffler, is it?" When I nodded yes, he continued, "Ms. Charles is ready to have this baby. Are you comfortable staying here for the birth?"

Again, I nodded and I felt Ryanne tighten her grip on my hand as she whispered, "Thank you."

The next few minutes were a blur but I remember the doctor telling Ryanne to push and I tried to support and encourage her the best I could. A short time later, the doctor carefully guided the baby into the world. He lifted her onto Ryanne's chest as the nurse massaged the baby to get her pinked up. They allowed Ryanne to look at her then carried her quickly to the exam table. It was such a beautiful moment, something I'd imagined for myself one day. My feelings were all twisted and confused and suddenly, I wanted to be away from it. This was not my wife, this was not my child and it wasn't my moment. I began to pull my hand free from Ryanne's but she held on tightly. "Please, don't leave me. I want to make sure she's okay."

I could only nod mutely as I watched the nurse measure and weigh the baby. After announcing she weighed a healthy five pounds three ounces, despite being born early, they wrapped her in a blanket, put a cap on her head to keep her warm, and then brought her to Ryanne. "Have you thought of any names?" I asked, trying to keep my voice from breaking with emotion.

She shook her head no. "I wanted to see her first. She's absolutely beautiful, isn't she?"

She really was. "Yes, she's probably the prettiest baby I've ever seen," I admitted.

Ryanne was glowing as she tipped her head forward to place a gentle kiss on her forehead. She seemed lost in thought so I took the opportunity to back away, prepared to step outside to give them some privacy. "Mason, where are you going?" she asked before I could slip out.

"I wanted to give you time with her. I'll be right outside," I said still heading for the door.

She shook her head, her eyes welling with tears. "No, please stay." Her voice broke with emotion. "I can't do this alone."

Slowly, I walked back to sit in the chair by the bed and watched as she unwrapped the baby to examine her fingers and toes. "She looks a lot like her daddy," she whispered. The baby stirred as Ryanne brushed her fingers across her chubby cheek. "I've had two names in my head since I found out she was going to be a girl but I needed to see her to know which one to pick."

She leaned in and whispered, "Happy birthday, Madison Grace."

"That's perfect." I whispered.

She smiled a sad smile. "I think Rusty would have liked that."

I nodded silently. A moment later, a nurse came to take the baby to the NICU to bathe her and perform some tests. Another nurse came to take care of Ryanne's needs so I took the opportunity to excuse myself. Once outside the door, I leaned against the wall and took a deep breath. I never expected the avalanche of emotions I was having. Seeing Ryanne with the baby had only reminded me of the disappointment I had at not having a family of my own. I'd buried all of those feelings after my divorce and accepted that I'd never get to experience any of the things I'd just been through tonight. I had to keep reminding myself that this wasn't my life. I was an outsider, an observer. The baby wasn't mine and neither was Ryanne. I felt guilty for even thinking of possessing them as thoughts of Rusty pounded in my brain. I needed to get some fresh air so I wandered down the hall.

"Mason!"

I turned to see Jolene rushing toward me. "Is everything okay? I just heard and headed straight over here."

"Yeah, she had the baby. They're both doing great." My voice sounded flat, emotionless.

Jolene studied me for a moment then said, "Um, well…can she have any visitors? I'd love to check in on her."

"Sure, she's in room 403. They're just cleaning her up so I was giving her some privacy."

Jolene rested her hand on my arm. "Are you okay? You look upset."

I gave her a weak smile. "Yeah, sure. I'm fine. It's just...sad."

She nodded. "Is she holding up okay?"

"She seems to be. She's a very strong woman."

We were interrupted by the nurse coming out of Ryanne's room. "You can go in, now. The baby's doing great and doesn't need to be admitted to the NICU. We're going to bring the baby back to her shortly." Jolene took my arm to lead me to the room but I balked.

"You go in. I'm going to make sure that nobody gives the press a heads-up that she's had the baby."

Reluctantly, she released my arm and went into the room after giving me a long look. It was obvious I was wearing my emotions on my sleeve and I needed to get myself back together. I made a quick call to Ryder to fill him in on the latest developments. He was at the house keeping an eye on Gage until Joey could relieve him. Joey Andrews was familiar with Gage having worked with him when Ryanne first signed on with Solitaire Security. This should have eased my mind but all I could think about was how scared Gage would be when he found out his mom was gone. Knowing I couldn't be with both of them at the same time was a horrible feeling but I knew Gage was in good hands. Out of the corner of my eye, I saw the nurse wheeling a bassinet down the hall. As she passed me, she nodded then opened Ryanne's door. Madison, who was sleeping peacefully, was now neatly wrapped like a burrito in a traditional hospital blanket with a tiny knit cap perched on her head. As if compelled, I followed them into the room.

Chapter 6

Ryanne

My head was spinning. So many things had happened so quickly, I felt as if I was caught in a whirlpool that was pulling me under. Rusty was gone. The realization that my husband wouldn't be sharing the birth of our baby hit me like a brick when my water broke. I needed someone so badly and I'd practically suffocated poor Mason with my needy, whiny requests to stay with me. He was my bodyguard and I'd insisted he stay by my side during my labor. What had I been thinking? He must be wondering what the hell he'd gotten himself into. If I'd had half a brain, I'd have seen the signs. He'd tried to leave the room but I'd insisted he come back. He'd held my hand throughout my labor but no doubt was wishing he could be anywhere else but there. Silent tears rolled down my cheeks as the nurse bustled around making sure I was clean and comfortable. She patted my hand and said,

"There, there. They'll be bringing your baby back to you in just a little bit."

More shame washed over me. I hadn't been focusing on my baby, only myself and my stupid behavior. A moment later, the door slowly swung open. Thinking it was Mason, I quickly wiped my cheeks with the back of my hand. Instead, it was Jolene.

"Is it okay if I come in?" she asked softly.

I nodded as I snatched a tissue from the box by my bed.

She came to stand beside the bed and took my hand in hers. "Congratulations," she said with a smile. "Mason filled me in."

"Is he still here?" I asked hopefully.

She nodded slowly. "Of course he is. He's your man."

"Excuse me?"

"Your man, your security. Where else would he be?"

I lay my head back on the pillow with a sigh. "Jolene, I'm a mess."

She perched on the side of my bed, still holding my hand. "You're not a mess," she said softly. "You've had a hell of a time and you're just overwhelmed. Your hormones have got to be wacky yet you have such emotional strength. I admire that about you."

Tears welled in my eyes. "I don't know what's happening to me."

She squeezed my hand gently. "Life is what's happening. You've had a terrible tragedy but you can't stop living because of it. You have Gage to think about and now this beautiful, little girl."

I smiled. "She is adorable. They should be bringing her back any time now. I named her Madison Grace."

"That's so beautiful," she whispered.

A moment later, the door opened and the nurse backed in pulling the bassinet in behind her, followed closely by Mason. His eyes met mine and I lost my breath for a moment. For the briefest second, I'd felt a strange

81

connection but then he looked away leaving me wondering what it was. No doubt it was the hormones, like Jolene had said.

The nurse picked Madison up and handed her to me. She was sleeping, her tiny hands tucked up beside her face. Her tiny lips were pursed, her brows furrowed. I touched her face gently with my index finger. At my touch, she opened her eyes and began gazing around. "She seems very content."

Jolene was leaning closer to see so I offered to let her hold Madison. She gingerly took her from my arms and slowly rocked her back and forth. Mason's eyes never left Madison and a strange feeling washed over me. Seeing how he was looking at her reminded me that I should have been experiencing this with Rusty and suddenly, I felt a stab of anger. It was so unfair. He would never hold his daughter, never see her grow up. Mason suddenly took me by the hand. "Are you okay? Do you need me to get the doctor?"

I shook my head. "No, I'm sorry. I'm just tired," I said making up a lame excuse for my behavior.

Mason studied my face so intently, I had to look away. "Ryanne, if you're worried about Gage, he's fine. Everything here is secure and the hospital understands the repercussions if any of your medical information is leaked. Madison will be here with you, not in the nursery where anyone could possibly take her picture to sell to the tabloids. You have nothing to worry about."

The anger ebbed and was replaced by exhaustion. "Thank you, for everything," I said softly. "I think I'll try to get some rest while Madison's asleep."

Jolene set Madison back into the bassinet then took my hand and giving it a squeeze, she said, "If you need to talk...about anything, call me."

I nodded mutely. She gathered her things, said goodbye to Mason, then left. He turned to follow her but stopped suddenly and turned to face me. "This is probably inappropriate for me to say to you but I feel I have to." His eyes softened. "This was one of the most amazing days of my life and I'm honored to have shared it with you. I know things have been tough for you. Please, if you need me for anything, I'm here. In our line of work, we're supposed to be prepared to lay down our lives for our clients and I can honestly say, for you or your family, I wouldn't hesitate one second."

A moment later, there came a knock and the door opened. The nurse peeked her head in. "I hope I'm not interrupting but I need to check your vitals and was going to see if you needed some help feeding her."

Mason backed to the door. "I'll be outside. Call me if you need anything." He walked out pulling the door shut behind him.

As the nurse busied herself checking my blood pressure, I thought about what he'd said. I'd never seen such emotion in his eyes before, or maybe I'd never taken the time to look. I'd become so dependent on him before and especially after Rusty died but I'd obviously been taking him for granted. He'd been so supportive through everything, especially through Madison's birth. It had seemed so natural to have him by my side, but now looking back, I'd put him in what had to be a difficult position. I couldn't imagine any guy, never mind an employee, doing everything he'd done for me. But that was the strangest part. He didn't feel like an employee. He was like a part of my family and was definitely someone I could trust with my life.

"Okay, Mrs. MacNeil, you're doing really well," the nurse said as she turned to pick up Madison. "I know you said you've had difficulty nursing in the past, is that why you wanted to bottle feed her?"

"Yes, I had trouble feeding my son, so I'd rather be safe than sorry."

She handed Madison to me and once I got her settled, I rubbed the bottle against her lips and she latched on hungrily. She drank most of the bottle. I managed to coax a healthy burp out of her and then she fell asleep again. The nurse placed her back in the bassinet then turned down the blinds and dimmed the lights.

"I'd suggest you get some rest, you're going to need it," she said with a smile.

My eyelids grew heavy and finally I could fight it no more. I closed my eyes.

"She's beautiful, babe." I opened my eyes to see Rusty standing over Madison's bassinet. "I told you she'd be as pretty as her momma."

"Rusty!" I cried. "What are you doing here?"

Giving me his crooked smile, he said, "I just stopped by to say hi. I'm watching over y'all every day. I loved the balloons, by the way."

I stared at him in disbelief. "But you died...you can't be real."

He leaned over the bassinet and gave Madison a soft kiss on her forehead. He straightened and then walked over to my bedside. I held out my hand to him but he didn't take it. "Baby, I need you to promise something. Promise me that you'll move on and live a happy life."

Tears sprang to my eyes. "Rusty, I can't. How can I do this without you?"

He glanced back at Madison then back at me, "You have so much to do. So much life to live. So much love still to give. Our children deserve happiness and the only way they'll get that is if you can move forward. I'll always *be watching over you. Promise me, Ryanne. I need to know you'll be okay."*

With tears spilling onto my cheeks, I managed to say, "I promise. Rusty, I'll always love you."

He smiled then took a step back. "Baby, I've got to go now."

"No, please don't leave me!" I cried reaching out to him.

I caught his hand and closing my eyes, pulled it against my cheek. "I need you."

"I'm not going anywhere." My eyes popped open to see Mason standing over my bed. I had his hand pressed to my tear-stained face. "Are you okay?" he asked, his eyes filled with concern.

"Mason," I whispered as I glanced around the room searching for any sign of Rusty. When the reality hit me that I'd been dreaming, I let go of his hand and the tears began to flow again. He gathered me into his arms and let me cry against his shirt until I couldn't find any more tears. Thankfully, he grabbed a tissue from the nightstand so I could dry my cheeks as he released me from his embrace.

I lay back against the pillows with a heavy sigh. "I'm so sorry. I must've been dreaming."

He nodded. "I heard you cry out and came right in to see if you were okay. You seemed very upset."

Taking another deep breath to calm myself, I started to tell him what I'd been dreaming about but something told me to keep it to myself. "I'm okay. It's probably just my crazy hormones playing with my mind."

"You're sure?" he asked with a frown.

"Yes, I'll be fine. Thanks again for everything."

His face grew serious. "Ryanne, I –" He was interrupted by a knock on the door. It opened slowly and my mom peeked her head in. "I'm here!" she whispered so she wouldn't wake the baby. She came in carrying a big bouquet of balloons and a stuffed teddy bear as big as herself. Mason took the things from her hands. "Thank you so much, Mason," she said with a smile. She then came rushing to my bedside. "How are you, darling?"

Out of the corner of my eye I watched as Mason set the bear down in a chair and carefully tied the balloons securely to the arm.

I put on my best smile for my mom. "I'm good. Just tired."

Mason backed out of the room and quietly closed the door.

"So, tell me. What's my beautiful granddaughter's name?" she asked as she turned to pull the bassinet closer to the bed.

"Madison Grace," I answered gazing over at my sweet girl who was sleeping peacefully.

My mom lightly brushed her finger across Madison's cheek and she turned toward it with a soft coo. "She's absolutely gorgeous." We sat there quietly watching her for a few minutes. "Honey, I know this has been a tough time for you but I want you to know how proud I am of you for holding it together like you have. I don't know what I would have done if I were in your situation."

"Thanks, Mom," I whispered trying to keep my composure. "I'm glad you're here."

She patted my hand and smiled. "Me too. Your dad says you can keep me for as long as you need me so do with me as you wish."

"I think between you and Mrs. Jamison, I'll have the best help I could possibly ask for," I said truthfully.

"That's what moms are for," she said giving my hand a reassuring squeeze.

Chapter 7

Mason

Ryanne and Madison came home from the hospital after only a couple of days. A statement was released to the press about the birth after she was already home, which prevented the onslaught of paparazzi. When they discovered she was home, however, they camped outside the gates of her house clamoring for a picture of the baby. Security was tightened to screen Ryanne's visitors. She had hundreds of people requesting to see the baby and some weren't even her friends at all. As a team, we checked everyone out before allowing them access to the house and had to scrutinize every package and gift that arrived for the baby. Rusty's best friend Lucas came bringing a four foot stuffed giraffe and a bouquet of flowers equal in size.

Madison was an absolute carbon copy of her mother and had to be one of the happiest babies I'd ever seen. Ryanne's mom, Cara, spent a lot of time with Gage freeing her up to spend time bonding with the baby. She didn't go out much for the first couple of weeks except for checkups for both herself and the baby so I really didn't have much to do except wait to be called upon.

Babies seem to grow overnight and soon four months had gone by. Watching Madison change every day, I found that the longing to have my own child had become a dull ache in my heart. It also made me realize that I was becoming too attached to them. It was an assignment, nothing more. I was their protection, not a part of their family. I'd always been able to draw the line between my personal feelings and work but now that line was blurred and it was confusing me. I didn't want to leave but I was also afraid to stay. The only thing I could do was take things one day at a time and hope my feelings didn't betray me.

One morning, I was making some coffee when Ryanne came into the kitchen. She grabbed a cup from the cupboard and waited for me to pour myself a cup. Her hair was damp and I could smell the fresh scent of her shampoo, which brought back the memory of my fantasy that now filled me with guilt. Taking a step back to clear my head, I felt her eyes on me.

"Mason, are you okay?"

With a quick nod, I began adding creamer to my coffee as I desperately tried to mask whatever she'd seen on my face.

She drank her coffee black so she walked over to the bar and slid onto a stool. "I need to talk to you about something," she said as she took a sip.

Without turning around, I said, "Okay, what's up?" It was so easy to be cool when I wasn't looking into her beautiful blue eyes.

"Well, the premiere of the movie is next month and I'll have to go to Los Angeles."

I stopped stirring and took a leisurely sip. "And?"

She got up off the stool and came to stand beside me. "I'm afraid it's going to be just the two of us. Kimberly is going to be handling all of my business from here and I certainly can't take the kids. Gage would probably be okay but traveling with a five month old would be pretty tricky. It's not fair to make them go with me. I really wish I didn't have to do this but it's all part of my contract."

Taking a deep breath, I turned to face her. "So, it's just me?"

She nodded. "Yes, the kids are going to stay here with my mom and Mrs. Jamison and Ryder's going to have a couple of the guys take care of things here while we're gone."

I swallowed hard. "How long are we going to be gone?" I asked.

"The entire trip is supposed to be two weeks but I'm hoping to condense it some. I have several guest appearances lined up and of course the premiere. You'll be my protection as well as my date for that particular event. Do you have a tux?"

I nodded. "Yeah, I've got one."

"Good, we'll be staying at the Beverly Wilshire and we'll have a driver at our disposal." When I began to speak, she cut me off. "I know what you're thinking. Kimberly booked us into adjoining suites. She knew you'd be concerned about the security side of things and want to be close by."

The thought of being alone with Ryanne for what could be two weeks was going to be the ultimate test of my will. The conflict must have shown on my face because she stepped toward me then rested her hand on my arm. "If you don't want to go, just say so."

Quickly, I shook my head. "Why would you think I don't want to go?"

She studied my face. "Honestly, you looked pretty miserable there for a moment so I figured you weren't real happy about it."

"I want to go. I'm sorry if I gave you any other impression."

With a sigh, she said, "Good, then it's settled. We leave on the fifteenth on the first flight out."

The month flew by filled with appointments, meetings and everyday stuff. Before I knew it, it was the day before the trip and the house was in chaos. Ryanne had waited until the last moment to pack so she was flying around the house like a banshee. I had already taken care of my things and to make things easier, I helped Cara and Mrs. Jamison with the kids by taking them outside to get fresh air.

The morning of our flight, I carried my bags down to the car that was waiting to take us to the airport. I quickly stowed them in the trunk then went back in to get Ryanne's. She was stuffing some shoes into her suitcase as I knocked on her open door.

"You almost ready?" I asked.

She struggled to zip the case but managed to get it closed then nodded. "Yes, I think I've cleaned out my entire closet."

As I easily hefted her bags, her eyes grew wide. "Mason, you make me look like a lightweight. I couldn't even move that bag."

I laughed as I carried them out of the room. "That's because I'm the man."

She snickered as she followed me downstairs. "Yeah, obviously."

She detoured into the kitchen where her mom was having an early breakfast with the kids. I could hear Gage crying and I felt a pang in my heart for the little guy. Recently, it had begun to really sink in that his dad wasn't coming back and he'd become very clingy to Ryanne. It was obvious that he was going to have a rough couple of weeks. Madison, however, was blissfully unaware and was only concerned with getting her bottle.

I went outside and waited by the car and soon Ryanne came running out dabbing her eyes with a tissue. She slipped into the backseat without a word and I climbed into the front seat next to the driver. We rode in silence to the airport then went directly to the VIP lounge. Several people were already waiting for the plane and I could hear the buzz of conversation start up as we found a seat near the huge glass windows. Several people had immediately recognized Ryanne and were either outright staring or sneaking glances when she wasn't looking. Taking a deep breath, I prepared myself to intercept anyone who decided they just had to talk to her.

A few minutes passed and then an older woman stood and began to walk over to us. Ryanne was gazing out the window, lost in thought so I cleared my throat to let her know someone was approaching. She turned to me with question in her eyes and then saw the woman who was almost at her side.

"Ms. Charles?" she asked timidly. Ryanne nodded silently with a smile.

"I just wanted to tell you how sorry I am for your loss. My husband passed away when I was about your age and I know how lost you must be feeling. You are such a lovely young woman and I wish nothing but the best for you in the future."

Ryanne smiled and held out her hand. "Thank you so much…"

"Mrs. Fletcher, but you can call me Agnes," she said taking her hand.

"Agnes, it is. Then you must call me Ryanne. It means so much to know that I'm not crazy for feeling the way I do."

An older man joined her and smiling said, "Agnes, you can leave the nice young lady alone now."

"Oh, Harry! I just wanted to say hello!" she said patting him on the arm. "Ryanne, this is my husband, Harry."

Harry looked me up and down and said with a chuckle, "So, is this your bodyguard?"

Ryanne smiled. "Agnes, Harry, this is Mason Leffler and yes, he's my bodyguard…security…whatever you'd like to call it. He's also my friend."

Harry held out his hand. "Nice to meet you, young fella. Did you play any football?"

We struck up a conversation about sports leaving the ladies to chat. Before we knew it, the plane was ready to board. We had first class tickets but as we were about to board, Ryanne saw a young couple obviously on their honeymoon as they were kissing and holding hands. She walked up to the ticket counter and inquired about where they were sitting and was told they were in coach so she asked if she could exchange our tickets for theirs. "Oh gosh, Mason, you don't mind, do you?" she asked.

"No, not at all. That's very generous of you. I'm sure they'll be thrilled." I followed her across the waiting area to the couple who, from their reaction, knew exactly who she was. With astonished expressions on their faces and their first class boarding passes in hand, they boarded along with Agnes and Harry, who gave her an appreciative nod. We boarded with the rest of the passengers and after finding our seats, heard the flight attendant recount what Ryanne had done which led to a round of applause from the rest of the passengers. She blushed so sweetly as she reluctantly stood and gave a little wave then dropped back into the seat beside me.

"I believe you just made some new friends," I said smiling.

"I didn't do anything remarkable," she said, still blushing. "I just wanted to give them a honeymoon to remember." She sat back and sighed. "Rusty and I never really had a normal honeymoon."

"If you don't mind my asking, how did you meet?" I asked.

She gave me a sad smile. "We met in the green room backstage at the Tanner Fox show and as we watched the show on the monitors, we talked and laughed. I'd heard of the feisty driver who'd just won the championship but his reputation was nothing like the man I met that day. Rusty was a race car driver with a public persona that was as cool as ice. In interviews, he was all business but as soon as they were finished, he turned into a big goofy kid. He kept that side of his personality for his private life and later when we were together, I appreciated him leaving the other Rusty at the track. Sweet Rusty was the guy I'd fallen in love with. After we finished taping the show, he'd confessed that he had no idea who I was when we first met. He thought I was one of the interns sent to entertain him while he waited but when they called me to the stage for my segment, he told me he'd watched in awe as I promoted my latest movie project. Following my interview, I stayed around to watch his and saw the public side of him as he nervously answered Tanner's questions. As highlights from his races, including his accidents were shown, I remember standing there in stunned disbelief. There were so many horrible wrecks where his car was practically demolished yet he always crawled out, raised his arms over his head, and pumped his fists to a frenzied crowd. After his segment finished, he came backstage to meet up with his security team and I boldly slipped him my number."

She gave me a sad smile. "He called later that night and we talked for hours. It was so easy and it scared me a little. I was so used to the pretentious Hollywood crowd but this was different, he was different. He was genuine and I liked that. One big drawback to our relationship was that our busy careers hindered spending any quality time together. I'd just begun working on a big-budget film that was, according to my agent, going to put me on the map. I was filming in California and Rusty was in Charlotte. He had just finished his race season and had some free time, so on an impulse, he flew to California to surprise me. It was wonderful. We spent the entire time together, secluded at my beach house, falling in love. Of course, I wanted the world to know we were together but my agent and my publicist advised against it. They were afraid that my relationship with Rusty would affect my career."

She closed her eyes and smiled. "Thank God, I didn't listen. We let the world in on our secret when we attended a charity event together and despite the concerns, the fans loved us together. He was the bad boy and I was America's sweetheart so we were definitely an interesting combination. After months of sneaking around we were finally free to be seen together. It was wonderful to be free. When my schedule allowed, I began to travel to his races and stood by his side as he climbed into his car always giving him a kiss for good luck. The fans were wonderful and embraced us as a couple which made the next step of getting married, a natural one. Rusty was racing in Nevada and asked me to come to see him race. Being so close to home, I drove out and when I arrived, I found both of our families there waiting for me. It turned out, Rusty had planned a surprise wedding and had down to the last detail. He'd picked out my dress with a little help from my stylist. It fit me perfectly and I loved the style because he knew me so well. We got married in a tiny chapel with our family and closest friends in attendance. We honeymooned in the RV parked at the track and then the next day, I had to head back to LA. He promised we'd have a proper honeymoon someday." She hesitated and took a deep breath. "I never imagined our time together would be so short."

I placed my hand on hers. "You loved a lifetime in the time you had together. Anyone would be envious of what you had together."

She turned to me. "You're right. I had a beautiful life."

"You mean you *have* a beautiful life. There's still plenty of life ahead."

She nodded. "All right, enough about me. Tell me, since you and your wife split, has there been anyone special?"

I shook my head. "I dated a dispatcher who worked with me in the department but she really wanted to get serious but I just couldn't."

"Did you leave LA to get away?"

"No, after I was shot…"

"Wait, what? You were shot?"

I nodded. "Yeah, I was called to a robbery in progress. I happened to be having lunch just around the corner so I was first on the scene and when I got out of my car, the guy came running from the store waving his gun. Immediately, I raised mine and yelled at him to drop his weapon but instead he fired off a shot and it hit me in the right shoulder. My gun flew out of my hand and to protect myself, I dropped down beside the car. He took off running down the street but another cruiser intercepted him and took him in custody. The trip to the hospital proved to be very enlightening. Suffice to say, while I was there, I found out she'd been cheating with a neurosurgeon who also happened to be married."

She shook her head. "Wow that really sucks."

I sighed. "Yeah, well after we divorced, they got married shortly after. I decided Los Angeles wasn't big enough for all of us so I moved to the east coast just to get away. Charlotte happened to be where I landed."

She smiled and patted my hand. "Well, I'm glad that's where you landed. Mason, I don't know what I would've done without your support through all this. It really means a lot to me."

"That's what I'm here for."

The flight attendant rolled a cart next to us. "Would either of you care for a beverage?"

Ryanne shook her head no, as did I. The flight attendant moved on and Ryanne turned her head to the side and closed her eyes. Within moments, she was fast asleep, so I opened my laptop and did some reports for Ryder while she slept. She looked so beautiful and I imagined what it would be like to wake up next to her every

105

morning. Guilt stabbed at my heart at the thought of Rusty and how much they'd loved each other, only to be torn apart by a horrible tragedy. She'd still be with him sharing a future filled with love and raising their beautiful children together.

She stirred and moaned and when I glanced over, I could see her face was contorted as if she were having a bad dream. Her hands were balled into fists and her jaw was tightly clenched. I touched her arm and she grabbed hold of my arm, her nails digging into my skin. "Ryanne," I said softly as I shook her gently.

She flinched and opened her eyes. She glanced down at her hand gripping me and quickly let go. "I'm so sorry. Did I hurt you?"

I shook my head. "No, are you okay?"

Tears welled up in her eyes. "I don't know. I haven't told anyone this but I've been having the same nightmare over and over ever since Rusty died. In my dream, I'm with him in the truck coming back from the race and we stop for gas. I run into the station to get a drink and when I come out, the truck's pulling away leaving me behind. I start to run, waving and calling out to him but he doesn't hear me. All of a sudden, I see the truck spin and flip over and over. I try to run to help him but I can't, it's like I'm stuck in quicksand. I guess I feel that if I were with him, I could have stopped it somehow."

"I know a lot of people don't believe in fate but I do. My grandpa always said that when it's your time, there's nothing you can do to stop it. He served in two wars and came home without a scratch but one day, he was walking out his back door, fell and hit his head against the wall. He never regained consciousness and died a couple of days later. His doctor told my gran that he was as healthy as a horse but he hit his head just right and that was it."

She sniffled and nodded. "Rusty always told me the same thing. He risked his life every time he got into his racecar and I worried the entire time he was racing but I never expected –" Her voice broke as she looked away.

"Ryanne, what happened was an accident and as hard as it is, you have to stay strong for your beautiful kids."

She smiled sadly. "They are pretty awesome, aren't they? I miss them already."

"Well, you'll be so busy while we're in LA that the time will fly by and before you know it, you'll be back home with them." Moments later, the captain made the announcement that we would soon be landing in Los Angeles.

As we made our way off the plane, we entered the main lobby of the airport and saw a man holding a card with Ryanne's name printed in big block letters. She waved to him and he tipped his hat. His name was Richard and he took our baggage claim tickets and retrieved our luggage then took them to a black limo parked at the curb. Out of the corner of my eye, I saw a couple of paparazzi standing near the door, no doubt on the prowl for any celebrity sightings. One of them glanced our way and his eyes grew wide. He elbowed his buddy and they came running over toward the car. I put myself between them and Ryanne allowing her to climb into the car.

"Ms. Charles, welcome to LA! How does it feel to be back?"

"Ms. Charles, look over here! Smile!"

Both photographers were pushing each other out of the way trying to get a good shot but I managed to block them. I quickly shut the door and since the windows were tinted, they couldn't get any more pictures. I climbed in the front with the driver and we sped away toward the hotel.

As Ryanne checked in, I gave the lobby a quick glance over. We were staying at one of the nicest hotels in Beverly Hills that was well acquainted with celebrity clients so I felt pretty comfortable with the accommodations.

"Mason!" I turned to see Ryanne waving to me.

"What's up?"

"Well, it seems that the room doesn't have an adjoining room."

I frowned. This wasn't good. I needed to be close by and as I started to say so, she started laughing.

"What's so funny?" I asked.

"Well, Kimberly booked me into the penthouse suite and basically, it's the entire top floor. It has three bedrooms so I guess you'll be sharing with me."

In any other circumstance, I would have been more than happy with that but as attracted as I was to Ryanne, once again, my common sense told me this was not a good idea. I cleared my throat to protest and was stopped by her fingers pressed against my lips.

"Mason, it'll be fine. I promise I'll give you your space. We share a house now, what's the difference? The penthouse is big and you'll have plenty of privacy."

She was forgetting one important fact. We were alone. No nanny, no kids, no one. Just us. But I kept my thoughts to myself. No need to complicate things. She obviously wasn't uncomfortable about it so why should I be? I simply needed to face the fact that she wasn't interested in me. She was still very much in love with her husband. I was just there to protect her – end of discussion.

I nodded curtly. "Okay, it's fine."

She frowned and seemed about to say something but instead turned and took the keycards, handing one to me. The bellhop rolled the cart loaded with our bags into the elevator which luckily was empty except for us. He inserted our keycard into a slot in the elevator and we went up to the penthouse. The doors opened into a small hallway which led to the enormous suite. There were spectacular panoramic views of Los Angeles in the distance from the terrace. The bellhop took the bags to the master bedroom which was almost the same size as Ryanne's at her home. It had a full bathroom with a marble soaking tub and oversized shower. I quickly scanned the room to make sure everything was secure and then followed him to my room. I had a room almost as big as the master which also had its own bathroom and equally amazing views. I threw my toiletries on the counter in the bathroom and quickly unpacked my suit and tuxedo from the garment bag to let any wrinkles ease out.

The bellhop rolled the cart toward the door and I saw Ryanne easily slip his gratuity into his palm. She smiled and thanked him and he flushed and grinned as he backed out the door. "My pleasure, Ms. Charles. If you need anything, my name is Kyle."

"Thank you, Kyle," she said walking him to the elevator. As the doors closed, she turned and leaned against the wall with a sigh. "Peace and quiet at last."

I chuckled. "Not for long. Kimberly gave me your itinerary and you've got interviews first thing tomorrow and then the movie premiere is starting at five so you have to be there for the red carpet by three."

She groaned. "Well, this is what I get paid for. I guess I shouldn't complain."

"It'll be over before you know it," I assured her.

She wandered into the suite and picked up the room service menu and started flipping through it. "So, what do you feel like doing for dinner?"

"I'm at your service. Whatever you feel like doing is fine with me." I walked over to stand behind her looking over her shoulder at the menu. I caught a whiff of her perfume and I took a moment to enjoy being so close to her. "What looks good?"

She ran her finger down the menu. "I think I'm in the mood for a burger. Pick one for me, I like anything." She handed the menu to me. "Order whatever you like. I think I'm going to take a bath to freshen up before it gets here."

I picked up the phone and called down for room service. I could hear her running the bath so I walked out onto the terrace to clear my head. It didn't work. I stood there watching the lights of Los Angeles begin to flicker to life, imagining Ryanne just a few feet away slipping into the fragrant bubbles of her bath. It had me literally going out of my mind. A short time later, I heard the chime of the elevator. I opened the door for the waiter who was pushing the dinner tray filled with covered dishes.

"Sir, the meal is complimentary as is the bottle of champagne," he said unloading the tray's contents onto the large dining table. "It's a gift from the management for Ms. Charles." He set the ice-filled champagne bucket onto a side table along with two crystal glasses.

"Thank you," I said slipping a gratuity into his waiting hand. "I'll be sure to let Ms. Charles know."

"You have a good night, sir." He backed out closing the door behind him.

"Mm, something smells delicious!"

Ryanne was coming from her room dressed in a satin robe, her hair tucked up into a towel. "I hope you don't mind, I didn't feel like getting dressed. Besides, you've seen me at my worst," she laughed.

I uncovered the dishes as she sat down in one of the chairs. "You don't get it do you?" I asked.

Puzzled, she frowned. "Get what?"

"You don't get how beautiful you are and that men are instantly attracted to you."

She scoffed. "I doubt that." I stared at her as she continued, "I mean, look at you. You're immune to me and you're with me every day." She looked directly into my eyes and I had to look away. She picked up her hamburger and mumbled, "Yep, that's what I thought."

I took a deep breath. "I'm a man and I'm just as attracted to you as anyone else but I have a professional line that I won't cross. I have a job to do and I know that you're off limits. Is that what you wanted to hear?"

Her jaw dropped open then she took a ragged breath. "Maybe I did."

We sat there in awkward silence and finally she stood and picked up the bottle of champagne. She poured herself a glass and raised her eyebrows to question if I wanted one, which I declined with a shake of my head. With a shrug, she picked up the glass and took a long drink then filled it up again. She sat back down and ate a few more bites of her dinner. "I think I'm going to go to bed. I've got a busy day tomorrow. Goodnight, Mason."

"Goodnight, Ryanne."

Chapter 8

Ryanne

I could hardly breathe as I shut the door behind me. My body was flushed and I needed to be alone to get myself together. I pulled the towel from my head and walked to the bathroom to comb my damp hair out. My reflection in the mirror shocked me. My cheeks were crimson, my eyes were sparkling. Mason was definitely attractive and on several occasions, I'd felt an attraction but had never seen any interest on his part, until tonight. I took another swallow of cold champagne but instead of cooling me off, it heightened the intensity of my feelings. I closed my eyes and let myself imagine Mason standing in front of me, his hands undoing the belt of my robe then sliding it free from my shoulders. His were eyes locked onto mine, his hands roaming over my bare skin…

The ringing of my phone made me just about jump out of my skin.

"Hello?" My voice cracked.

"Ms. Charles, it's the front desk. You have a package that was delivered just a few minutes ago."

I swallowed hard trying to regain my composure. "Oh well, I'm in for the night. I'll just get it in the morning but thank you for letting me know."

"Yes, ma'am. Not a problem. We'll make sure we don't disturb you for the rest of the evening."

"Thank you." I hung up the phone then heard Mason's bedroom door close. I dropped into the chair next to my bed and covered my face with my hands. He was only a few feet away and we were all alone. I wanted Mason. I sat there for what seemed like an eternity wrestling with whether or not to act on it and finally I made a decision. As quietly as possible, I opened my door and stepped out into the short hallway. Steeling myself, I was prepared to knock but suddenly stopped short. What was I doing? Was I going to sleep with Mason just to quench some need? This would only complicate our relationship. My common sense told me to turn around and head back to my room pronto. I spun around to make a quick escape but my heart skipped a beat when I heard his door open behind me.

"Is everything okay?" The rumble of his voice sent shivers up my spine.

Flustered, I stammered, "Uh, yeah…" As my eyes traveled from his confused face down to his bare, rock-hard chest, I swallowed hard. He was dressed only in a pair of gray shorts that hung low on his slim hips. His long hair was loose and hung around his face in waves. We'd lived in the same house for months but I'd never seen him in so little and I couldn't tear my eyes away. He was incredible in every sense of the word. I bit my lip nervously then slowly brought my eyes up to meet his.

"Ryanne, is there something you *want*?" His voice dropped to a growl causing me to swallow hard.

I shook my head. "No, this was a bad idea," I mumbled as I turned to go but then felt his hand wrap around my arm as he pulled me back to face him. He didn't say a word, only pulled me closer until I could feel the heat from his skin searing through the thin silky material. I stumbled forward as if in a trance, unable look away from his icy blue eyes. His hand cupped the nape of my neck sending shivers down my body and my lips parted as he pulled me even closer. As I breathed in and I closed my eyes, I could detect the faint scent of his aftershave. I stood on my toes to bring my lips to his but then nothing happened. My eyes fluttered open and I found him studying me intently.

"Are you sure?" he whispered the words and I could feel his warm breath on my skin.

At that moment, that was the only thing I was sure about. I nodded. "Yes," I said softly.

With a moan, he captured my mouth with his. The softness of his lips rendered me breathless as did the playful dart of his tongue against mine. His fingers firmly gripped the nape of my neck as his other arm tightened around my waist like a vise, locking me tightly to him. Instinctively, my arms wrapped around his shoulders and my fingers tangled into his thick hair. He backed into the room pulling me with him and I clung to him, unable to break away from the soul-searing kiss I'd been yearning for.

With ease, he untied my robe and slipped it from my naked body and instead of feeling self-conscious, I felt perfectly at ease. He took a step back and I immediately missed the warmth of his skin. "You're spectacular," he whispered as his eyes traveled up and down my body. "You don't know how long I've wanted this."

Taking his hand in mine, I pulled him back to me. Without a word, I tugged at his shorts until they dropped to the floor. He gathered me into his arms and pressed his lips against mine, stealing my breath once again. Laying me gently on the bed, he trailed his fingers across my forehead pushing my hair away from my eyes.

I cupped his cheek with my hand, feeling the gruff of his beard against my skin. He turned his face into my palm and placed several gentle kisses there before kissing my lips just as softly. As we lay tangled together, my hands trailed down his body and I noticed the hint of a smile on his face.

He eased me onto my back then began to stroke my cheek with his thumb while gently holding my face toward him. He deliberately slid his fingertips down my body slowly, delighting in my response as my back arched and I gasped and called out his name.

I desperately wanted to touch him too but he shook his head no. "Not yet," he said as he pressed a kiss to my hip. "Just enjoy."

I savored every touch and kiss he gently placed on my body. I felt a huge wave of emotion wash over me. As we made love, my body responded to his touch as if we'd always been lovers, which was an amazing feeling but it also scared the hell out of me. I shook the fear from my head and held on to him tightly as waves of delicious sensations began to take me higher and higher until the world exploded. Every nerve in my body was tingling and as I opened my eyes, I found his intently looking into mine. Again, he gave me that smile. He kissed me again and within moments, I was once again losing my senses but this time, I wasn't alone. He was holding me tightly, his kiss becoming more and more demanding then his body suddenly tensed and he cried out my name. His husky cry ignited my passion even more and I spun out of control digging my nails into his back as I cried out against his shoulder.

Moments later, we lay side by side, both too exhausted to move. Tucked in the crook of his arm, I snuggled against him, softly running my hand across his chest. He feathered kisses across my forehead as he murmured sweet nothings. It felt so good to be in his arms. He pulled the covers up over the both of us and soon, we were fast asleep.

I cracked my eyelids open and felt a splitting headache roar through my head as the sunlight streamed onto my face. I began to move then realized I wasn't in my own bed. I turned to see Mason fast asleep next to me.

I groaned inwardly. What had I done? Bits and pieces of the night before came back to me but it was all fuzzy. I'd always been a lightweight when it came to champagne and obviously, I'd had a little too much. I could remember having crazy inappropriate thoughts about Mason but that's where I seemed to lose track. I strained my brain trying to remember exactly how I ended up in his bed but instead I got a searing pain through my skull. My mouth felt like I'd been gargling cotton balls and my breath had an odor that was downright unpleasant. I lifted the covers and saw we were both naked, as I had

122

suspected. My stomach lurched with guilt as Rusty's face loomed in my mind and I had to fight back tears. I managed to slide out of bed without disturbing Mason then grabbed my robe from the floor. Quickly, I slipped it on and as quietly as possible, I crept out of his room and then dashed back to my own and locked the door.

With my head pounding like a jackhammer, I climbed in the shower turning the water as hot as I could stand it, trying to clear my thoughts. Resting my head against the cool tiles eased the ache a little but that was when the tears began to cascade down my cheeks. I couldn't blame the alcohol for this. The attraction I'd had for Mason was there before I even took my first sip, it just gave me the courage to act on it. The worst thing about the whole situation was that I felt as if I'd betrayed my husband. Until last night, Rusty had been the only man I'd ever been with and even though he was gone, the guilt was almost unbearable. Sobs wracked my body as I cried for everything I'd had and lost. I also felt shame for having used Mason because now it was only going to complicate things between us.

When I'd finally cried myself out, I climbed from the shower and wrapped myself in a towel. I could hear Mason moving around in the suite and a sickening knot formed in my gut at the thought of facing him after what I'd done. The only blessing was that I had a busy day ahead and if I timed it right, I could avoid being alone with him. After dressing, I took extra time to fix my hair and makeup, stalling until I heard a knock at the suite door and the entertainment reporter and his crew came in. A moment later, Mason knocked on my door.

"Ryanne? Zane Baxter from Celebrity Stalker is here for your ten o'clock interview."

I cleared my throat and with a shaky voice called back, "Be there in a couple of minutes."

Taking one last look in the mirror, I opened my door to find him still standing there. "Are you okay?" he asked with concern.

I nodded and stepped around him. "Yes, I'm fine, thank you."

I could feel his eyes following me as I greeted Zane and his crew. They had set up a couple of chairs on the terrace along with the lighting and sound. Zane began to give me an overview of some of the questions that mainly centered on the new movie. The sound man clipped a microphone to the strap of my sundress and Zane took his seat across from me. When they were all ready to begin taping, he asked me the first question.

"So, Ryanne, first let me offer my sincere condolences on the loss of your husband, Rusty. I know you've been dealing with some serious and painful issues and I want you to know that we at Celebrity Stalker all send our best."

He'd never mentioned that he'd start out with mentioning Rusty and it threw me off guard. I swallowed hard trying to keep my composure and somehow managed to plaster a fake smile on my face. "Thank you, Zane. It has been hard."

"We understand you're in Los Angeles for the premiere of your new movie "War of Love" which is set during the Civil War. Do you feel a stronger connection to your character Victoria now that you're a widow?"

My mouth fell open. "Excuse me?" I stammered.

"Let me rephrase that. We understand that your character becomes a widow and we were wondering if you felt a closer connection to her now," he asked leaning closer.

"Zane, I understood the question the first time and I really don't feel it's appropriate."

He nodded seriously. "Of course. My apologies, we'll move on. Okay, it's been a few months since you…um…how can I phrase this…became single? Have you thought of finding love again?"

My face flushed crimson as I stared at him incredulously. "Are you freaking serious?" I blurted. "I didn't 'become single', my husband died. I think this whole line of questioning is very disrespectful and frankly Zane, I'm disappointed in you." I yanked the microphone from my dress and flung it onto the floor before fleeing to my room.

I slammed my door and threw myself onto my bed in anger. I knew that I was going to be scrutinized but I had no idea how brutal it was going to be. Suddenly, I heard a commotion in the suite.

"You son of a bitch. You think you can come in here and upset her like that?" It was Mason.

Zane's reply was muffled then I heard a loud bang and glass breaking then the suite door slammed shut. I lay there with my face buried in my pillow until I heard a soft knock at my door.

"You okay?" Mason asked. When I didn't answer, he slowly opened the door. "Ryanne, he's gone. I threw his ass out."

I lifted my face from the pillow and wiped my eyes. "Thank you, I didn't know what to say."

He sat beside me on the bed and brushed my damp hair from my eyes. "People can be insensitive. I'm sorry you had to go through that."

He handed me a tissue and I blew my nose. "I guess I'm going to have to get used to questions like that. It threw me off, I guess."

After several moments of awkward silence, I glanced over at the clock and jumped up. "Oh gosh, look at the time, I've got to start getting ready for the premiere."

It seemed as if Mason wanted to say something but instead, he stood and walked out of the room. I grabbed a quick shower and as I was drying off, I heard voices in the suite. A moment later, a light knock fell upon the door. "Ms. Charles? I'm here to do your hair and makeup for tonight." I wrapped myself in a robe and opened the door to find a pretty blonde woman wearing jeans and a tank top standing outside. She smiled and gave a small wave. "I'm Brylee Sommers."

I returned the smile. "Pleased to meet you, and it's Ryanne." I stood back to let her enter and she rolled a couple of bags into the room. She pulled a chair over for me to sit and unpacked her makeup and styling products. My hair was still damp so she combed it out and as she worked, she talked about how gorgeous my hair was and how smooth my skin was. She was such a sweet person and I could tell she was very outgoing. She worked quickly and in no time had my hair styled into loose curls. She then began to apply my makeup and we had such a great time talking, the time flew by. When she finished, she handed me a mirror and I gave my appearance a final look over. She had done an amazing job and I was very pleased.

The dress I'd chosen to wear was a form-fitting silver sequined long gown which I paired with a pair of silver sandals. My jewelry was minimal and my only accessory was a small silver clutch.

"Ryanne," Mason called from the hallway. "It's time to go."

I stepped out of my room and my eyes fell upon one of the most stunning men I'd ever seen. Mason was wearing a black tuxedo with the traditional bowtie but what made it so perfect was the fit. It was tailored perfectly showcasing his broad shoulders and his trim waist. His hair was slicked back into a ponytail and I noticed he'd left just the hint of scruff on his cheeks. He also smelled as incredible as he looked. He looked as if he'd stepped off the page of a high fashion magazine. As I approached, he turned and his eyes locked onto mine before traveling leisurely down the length of my body. I saw the hint of a smile come to his lips.

My mind was a whirlwind of emotions. This beautiful man was standing in front of me, a man I'd made love to only hours before, but in the back of my mind, all I could think about was how recklessly I'd behaved. My heart was screaming for love but my head was telling me that I was wrong for wanting someone else. My thoughts were interrupted by Mason taking my hand then pulling it to his lips. "You are absolutely the most beautiful woman I've ever seen," he murmured against my skin.

Taking a deep breath, I gave him a shy smile. "Thank you," I whispered. He nodded then released my hand. He settled his hand on the small of my back and led me to the elevator. "Mason, I…"

He shook his head. "No, please don't say anything. I know what my boundaries are in public and I accept them."

His jaw was set and his expression guarded. We stepped into the elevator and I was acutely aware of how close he was to me and how powerful his body was. I closed my eyes and images from our night together began to flash through my mind causing my body to flush. He stepped closer to me until I could feel his breath against my bare neck. He didn't say a word, and it was literally driving me insane.

The elevator chimed our arrival in the lobby and the doors opened to reveal several paparazzi waiting by the doors. "Ms. Charles, over here!" One photographer called out.

"Ms. Charles, you look spectacular!"

Mason placed his hand on the small of my back to quickly lead me out of the lobby and into the waiting limo.

As we arrived in front of the theater, the flashes from the cameras combined with the eager screams from the crowd pushed my adrenaline through the roof. The fans, who'd been waiting for hours were eagerly waiting for any acknowledgement from the arriving stars of the movie and so I slowly made my way down the red carpet to accommodate them. I stopped for pictures, signed photos, and shook hands which delighted and also satisfied them. Despite the steady screaming, I could make out some of what they were saying.

"You are so beautiful!"

"Ryanne!"

"Ms. Charles, I love you!"

When I heard that, I turned to scan the crowd and managed to catch a glimpse of a pencil thin man standing right behind a woman who was screaming and waving an autograph book. What caught my eye was that he was wearing a baseball cap with Rusty's car number on it and also one of his team jackets. His eyes zeroed in on me and I felt an uneasy chill from his scrutiny.

A reporter from one of the entertainment shows was waiting to conduct a red carpet interview so I quickly answered a few questions and then was escorted to the theater doors. I suddenly realized that Mason and I had become separated and I began to panic as the crowds tried to surge around me trying to grab at me as I passed. The crowd was so exuberant that they began to push past the barricades and into the security guards who were unable to hold them back. The screams became louder as people began to become crushed by the strength of the crowd behind them. I looked ahead of me and saw the door to the theater had become blocked. Suddenly, Mason came out of nowhere, took me by the arm and forced his way through the crowd. With a mighty push, he threw open the doors. My body was trembling with fright and I could barely catch my breath. Mason cupped my face in his strong hands. "Are you okay?" he asked as his eyes searched my face.

With a hitching breath, I managed to say, "Yes, I think so. That was scary."

A moment later, a security guard came bursting through the doors. "Ms. Charles, I'm so sorry. We thought we had enough security but the crowd was bigger than we expected. Are you injured?"

As Mason put his arm protectively around me, I shook my head no. Leaving the guard to work on the crowd control, Mason led me to my reserved seat in the theater. After a few minutes, I began to calm down and breathe more normally. He sat holding my icy cold hands in his, concern written all over his face.

Finally, I said, "Mason, thank you so much."

He smiled and brushed the hair from my eyes. "Just doing my job."

Mason looked over my shoulder and backed away from me. I soon discovered it was because my co-stars, Ty Johnstone and Melodie Kramer had arrived. They had played a couple onscreen and ended up falling in love off screen as well and had just gotten married in Vegas. They took their seats next to mine and we exchanged hellos just as the movie began.

For the next two hours, my heart literally broke. Watching my character become a widow onscreen hammered home my own real-life situation. Tears began to stream down my cheeks as Victoria made her way through the dozens of wounded soldiers searching yet praying that her husband wasn't among the dead only to find his lifeless body on a litter in the back corner.

The air became thick and I found it hard to breathe. My survival instincts kicked in and I bolted from the theater. A rush of cold air hit me in the face as I pushed through the doors. Looking to the right, I saw the lobby full of reporters milling around waiting for interviews. When I looked left, there was a long empty hallway. In an effort to avoid attention, I quietly made my way down the hallway and found a small alcove I could duck into.

Leaning against the wall, I closed my eyes and tried to catch my breath. I never thought seeing myself become a widow onscreen would hit me as hard as it did. All of the emotions I'd kept buried down deep came crashing down around me and the feeling was overwhelming. Tears seeped from my tightly clenched eyes as I bit my bottom lip to keep myself from losing it.

"Ryanne?" I heard Mason call out softly. "Are you okay?"

I didn't respond, I just couldn't. A moment later I heard him say, "There you are. Listen, I can get you out of the theater if you want to leave."

Swallowing hard to compose myself, I said, "Yes, I need to go."

He eased around the corner into the alcove and took me by the hand to lead me out of a side door where the car was waiting by the curb. A reporter, who'd gone around to the side of the building to smoke saw us come out and tried to intercept me but Mason pushed him out of the way and quickly helped me into the car. We sped away and headed back to the hotel in silence.

Luckily, when we arrived, there were only a few guests in the lobby so we were able to make our way to the elevators without being spotted. Once inside the suite, I bolted for my room but Mason caught me by the arm.

"Talk to me. What's going on? I have a feeling this isn't all about the movie."

A sob escaped my lips. "Mason, I can't do this. I just can't. Please, let me go." I tried to pull my arm free but he wouldn't let go. He spun me toward him, and I found myself looking up into his eyes, which were filled with confusion.

"What can't you do? A relationship? I never asked for that. I was content to love you from a distance but you were the one who came knocking at my door. Dammit! You came to me!"

Tears began to stream down my cheeks as I struggled to escape. "Mason, it was a mistake! I shouldn't have used you! I needed someone and you were here!"

His jaw clenched. "You mean to tell me that if anyone else had been working with you on this trip that you would've seduced them?"

136

Flushing with shame, I pulled my arm free then ran into my room, locking the door behind me. Throwing myself onto the bed, I cried into my pillow until I fell into an exhausted sleep.

Chapter 9

Mason

The sound of Ryanne sobbing was more than I could take. I hadn't meant to yell and I cringed as I recalled the look on her face when I'd implied she'd sleep with anyone who worked with her. I took the beautiful night we'd spent together and cheapened it into a one-night stand. Pulling my phone from my pocket, I walked into my bedroom, shut the door and called Ryder.

"Hey, man, what's up?"

"Ryder, I need to you replace me." I was greeted with silence. "Are you there?"

He sighed. "Yeah, I'm here. What happened?"

I blew out a breath. "I need to get out of here. Can you send someone?"

"Mason, I'm not going to ask how but I want you to think this through. Are you sure you want to be replaced?"

I tucked the phone against my cheek and shoulder as I threw my clothes into my bag. "Yeah, I'm sure."

"All right, let me see what I can do." He hung up and I tossed the phone onto the bed next to my bag. I was gathering my things from the bathroom when I heard my phone ring.

"Mason, I'm sending Joey on the red-eye. He'll be there at midnight your time. Can you arrange for a car to pick him up?"

"Yeah, I'll take care of it. Thanks, Ryder."

Ryder sighed. "When you get back, we need to talk. Agreed?"

"Sure thing, Boss."

I hung up then called the car service to arrange for Joey's pick up at the airport. I was glad Ryder was sending Joey. He'd worked with Ryanne before and had a good relationship with Gage. When I thought of not seeing Ryanne or Gage again, it made me sad but I knew this was the right way to handle things. She didn't need me messing up her life and all I could do was hope that one day she'd find love again.

I lay down on the bed and flipped on the TV to pass the time.

A few hours later, I got the call from the front desk that he'd arrived so I went down to the lobby to escort him up. I set him up in the spare room and briefed him on Ryanne's schedule for the rest of the week. He kept looking at me strangely but didn't ask any questions. That was fine by me. I didn't even want to begin to try to explain. I gathered my bags and started to the door of the suite but stopped outside Ryanne's door to listen. The crying had stopped leaving only silence. I touched the door gently and said, "Goodbye."

The flight I was booked on wasn't until six in the morning but I went to the airport anyway and made myself comfortable in a hard plastic seat near the departure gate. I managed to catch a nap and soon it was time to board. I quickly found my seat and was about to turn off my phone when it began to ring. I glanced at it and saw it was

Ryanne. I sat there staring at it until it went to voicemail and then I turned it off.

Pulling my headphones from my bag, I hooked up my iPod and lost myself in my music for the entire flight. When we arrived in Charlotte, Ryder was waiting at the gate to pick me up. He didn't say much, just asked about the flight and if I'd gotten Joey settled in okay. We climbed into his SUV and that was when I realized that I wouldn't be going back to Ryanne's house.

"Crap…" I groaned.

Ryder pulled into the traffic and glanced over at me. "What's up?"

"Can you take me to my apartment? I guess I'll just have to make arrangements to get my things from the house later."

He nodded. "I can do that. And when you're ready to tell me why you had to quit this job, I'm here to listen."

I lay my head back against the headrest. "It's complicated, Boss. I'm not sure if I could ever explain."

We rode the rest of the way in silence and as I unlocked the door of my apartment and walked in, the silence hit me. I'd become so used to the sound of Gage playing and Madison's giggles. I had done what I'd sworn I would never do. I had crossed the line. I'd begun to believe there was a future with Ryanne and been living a dream. This was a job and I had forgotten to keep it that way.

I closed my eyes and pictured Ryanne at my bedroom door dressed in her satin robe. Her eyes were shining and her cheeks had a flush which was either from the champagne or from embarrassment because I could tell she was on the verge of bolting back to her room. Her sweet fragrance was mouthwatering and I took a deep breath in to enjoy it. She bit her bottom lip nervously, swallowed hard then took a tiny step backwards.

When I asked what she wanted, her eyes grew wide, she mumbled something and turned to leave but I couldn't let her just leave. I had to see if she wanted me and when I pulled her back to me, I knew as her lips parted for mine. Her body was pressed tightly against mine and I felt her hands slip around my waist. My hand tangled into her hair pulling her hungry mouth to mine but at the last moment, I hesitated. I needed to know if she really knew what she was about to do. I wanted there to be no regrets, nothing between us. As she said yes, I let all the passion I'd been holding back loose in a kiss that had left us both breathless and weak in the knees. I knew this was a very sensitive time for her and so I let her show me how far she was willing to go. I almost expected things to be awkward at first, as if we were two teenagers trying to figure things out but instead, there was an ease with which we made love, as if we'd always been lovers. When she'd fallen asleep in my arms, I'd been the happiest man on earth.

The next morning, I knew right away that something had changed. The only conclusion I could come to was that she'd been hit by guilt. She went out of her way to avoid me and when we were together, it was as if a wall had been built between us. I immediately had regretted that anything had happened between us but it was too late for that. The only hope I had was that it was something that she'd eventually work through and things would be okay with us again.

As soon as the movie started, I saw the stricken look on her face and knew I'd lost her. The way she'd stiffened at the scenes where the widow faces her husband's death, I knew she was reliving it and at the same time, beating herself up for betraying her husband. My heart wrenched as I saw tears slip from her eyes as she bolted from the theater and when I'd found her hiding from the press down the hallway, I saw only sadness and loss in her eyes. We rode back to the hotel in silence and finally, I couldn't take it anymore. I had to know even if it would end up breaking my heart.

Leaving her this morning without explanation was probably the crappiest thing in the world to do but also was probably the best way to handle things. She didn't need me complicating her life. She was a famous and successful woman who didn't need to lower her standards to an ex-cop/bodyguard like me. I groaned and threw myself onto the bed. The time change was catching up with me and the lack of sleep was wearing on my brain. I got up, shut my phone off, closed the blinds to darken the room and crashed into a deep sleep.

A loud banging on my apartment door startled me awake and I stumbled out of the bedroom glancing at the clock as I passed by. It was late and I realized that I'd been asleep for over ten hours. I yanked open the door to find Ryder leaning against the door frame.

"So, you are alive," he said brushing by me to come in. "Did you ever think that someone might need to get in touch with you? What'd you do, turn off your phone?"

I sighed. "Yeah, I needed to be unavailable. Why're you looking for me? You knew exactly where you left me."

He opened my fridge and grabbed a soda. "Well, Mason, it seems we have a problem." He popped the top and took a long drink.

I perched on the bar stool next to my kitchen counter. "A problem? What are you talking about?"

He shook his head and smiled. "Well, I had to send Joey to work security for Ryanne and now my sister-in-law is mad at me! Apparently, Olivia's been seeing him on the sly and is NOT happy that he's going to be working out of town."

I was confused. "Why would she be upset? He's not going to be gone forever."

Ryder took another swallow of his soda. "You know how it is when a relationship is new, there are always bumps in the road. Care to tell me about yours?"

I groaned and dropped my forehead against the counter. "Ryder, I can't."

When I was met with silence, I turned my head to glance over at him and he was studying me closely. "Mason, I admire that you're keeping certain parts of your assignment confidential but I have to know if this is a permanent reassignment or just temporary."

I lifted my head and rubbed my temples. "It's permanent. I think Ryanne would be better off with a different security detail. Maybe not Joey permanently, but someone other than me."

He tossed his can into the recyclables and slapped me on the shoulder. "You've got it bad, man. I'm not blind. She's a beautiful person and she's worth fighting for. If you give up now, you're a fool."

I shook my head. "I have no choice, Ryder. I'm competing against a ghost. He was a perfect husband. Maybe if he'd been a piece of crap and left her for someone else, it would have been easier but he didn't. He loved her until his dying breath and that deserves respect. Ryanne isn't ready to move on and I'm not going to make her life miserable by following her around like a lovesick puppy. The choice is hers."

Ryder walked over to the door and placed his hand on the knob. "Look, you need to get yourself together. Come in tomorrow and I'll figure out where to assign you."

He opened the door and with one last glance, pulled it shut behind him.

I couldn't sleep so I got in my Charger and drove around town. I found a Krispy Kreme donut place with their familiar red sign lit up and I turned in. I ordered a few of their delicious donuts and a hot cup of decaf coffee and sat by the window to watch the lights of the city. It suddenly occurred to me that my phone was still off so I turned it on and saw several texts and missed calls light up my screen. They were mostly from Ryanne with only a couple from Ryder sent right before he showed up at my door. I skimmed through and could see the same message over and over from Ryanne. CALL ME MASON was the most popular one and even a DON'T DO THIS was thrown in a couple of times. I touched the screen to reply but then found that I couldn't find any words. I'd said everything I needed to say and she'd made it clear that what had happened between us was just a one-time thing. She wasn't ready and she'd made that abundantly clear. I turned my phone back off, finished my coffee and the last bite of my donut and drove back home to try to get some sleep.

The next morning, I dragged myself into the shower, shaved and grabbed a big mug of coffee. The caffeine gave me the boost I needed to make it to the office. The doorman Kris waved me through with a smile and a nod. A few people were waiting for the elevator and I noticed their conversation dried up as I approached. I laughed to myself knowing that it had to be my appearance that was the cause. Ryanne had always commented that the ladies were checking me out but I had the feeling that most people weren't sure if I was dangerous or not. Mentally, I kicked myself in the ass for thinking of Ryanne again. It was time to get the game face on and tackle a new assignment. When the elevator doors opened, everyone boarded and I noticed that they'd pressed the button for the fourteenth floor which was the same one our office was located on. We rode in silence until we reached our destination and I noticed everyone made a hasty exit leaving me for last. They headed toward the office that belonged to my boss's wife, Jolene. Jolene Brisson was a successful fashion designer and always had famous and prestigious clients going in and out of her office. In fact, that was where I met Ryanne. Damn, there she was again, right back in the front of my mind. Shaking my head to clear my thoughts, I opened the door to our office and found Darryl Yancy, one of my co-workers working on the computer at the reception desk.

"Well, lookie what we have here," he rumbled and stood to shake my hand. "How've you been, man?"

Darryl was the only man in our office who towered over me. He was at least six-five and weighed an easy two-fifty.

"I've been good. Just got back in town and ready to get to work."

He frowned. "Okay…not my business."

I shrugged. "I know, I had a great assignment and now I'm out. Things happen."

He dropped into the chair and leaned back. "Well, if you need to talk, I've got two ears. Ryder's in his office and I've got to finish up this report and then I'll be right there." He leaned forward and started pecking the keyboard as I knocked on Ryder's door.

"Come in," he called out.

I opened the door to find Ryder standing at the window looking out over the Charlotte skyline. He turned and smiled when he saw me. "Good morning. Are you feeling better?"

I sat in the plush leather visitor's chair then crossed my ankle over my knee. "Yeah, I think so."

He walked over to his desk and picked up a folder. "Mason, I have to tell you, Ryanne's pretty upset. She called me last night when you wouldn't return her calls and I explained that you'd shut everything down but you know that's not going to fix things. You need to call her or text or even email her. Something. You walked out on an assignment and whatever your reasons were, she's hurt."

I sighed. "Ryder, I know you're not stupid. Something happened that shouldn't have and she regretted it. End of story. I crossed a line and I need to back away from the situation before it gets worse."

He sat on the edge of his desk. "So, she regretted it…and you obviously didn't."

"Right. I've had it bad for her since day one but I kept myself professional, especially since she was married. When Rusty died, it was the most horrible thing ever but in the back of my mind, I was thinking about the fact that she was available. Believe me, my conscience and I had some knock-down, drag outs about this and I managed to keep my distance. When we went to California, we were away from all the memories of her past and she seemed to be enjoying being back in the spotlight. I won't get into particulars but basically, she seemed ready to move on…with me. That all changed after the movie premiere. The part she'd played in that movie was so eerily similar to her real life situation that it freaked her out. She grew distant almost immediately and when I tried to talk to her, she made it clear that whatever had happened had been a huge mistake. I don't need to be hit over the head with things, I catch on quick. So, I called you to get a replacement and made myself scarce."

Ryder folded his arms. "So, you didn't give her time to process everything, you just bailed."

I felt a wash of shame come over me. "No, I did what was best for her."

With a sigh, Ryder handed me the folder. "Your assignment is a senator's son, Aaron Fleming. He's just received a pretty handsome scholarship and someone doesn't like it. He's received some threatening emails implying that he shouldn't be getting a free ride in college since his mother works for the government. You're going to be protecting him round the clock until the police trace the emails and get the person responsible."

Inwardly, I groaned. A spoiled college kid? Great.
I took the folder and quickly flipped through. From my
first impression, he was a clean-cut kid and had pretty
good grades as well. I stood and held out my hand.
"Thanks for being so understanding."

Ryder gripped it tightly. "Mason, just remember,
you can have that job back anytime."

I nodded. "Thanks."

Chapter 10

Ryanne

The one thing I didn't want to happen actually happened. Mason left and he left without telling me.

Now that he was gone and Joey was here, I felt so alone. Joey was nice but we'd never spent any real time together and with Mason it was different. He'd become so important in my life and because I'd had some crazy hormone attack, I ruined our relationship. He was my friend and knew me better than I knew myself sometimes. It was eerie how he anticipated my moves and I'd explained it away as being part of his job but now I realized that it was more than that. He really did care for me and had put his heart on the line by taking me into his bed. The worst part was that I was using Rusty as an excuse. Being lonely wasn't the reason I slept with Mason. That would have been too easy. I was attracted to him, both physically and emotionally but too stubborn to

154

admit it. I was more worried about what people would think if I moved on rather than focusing on my own feelings. I needed to talk to him and tell him these things but now he was gone and ignoring my calls and texts. At least I knew where he was. Ryder was kind enough to let me know that. Jolene called me and we talked for a while and before long, I was crying and incoherent.

"Jolene, am I wrong for feeling this way? For feeling that I'm betraying my husband?" I sobbed.

"Ryanne, you're the only judge of your heart. What happened to Rusty was an accident, a tragic one, but still an accident. Unfortunately, the ones who suffer are the ones left behind. Rusty knew a beautiful love until the day he died and you deserve the same. Mason's a good man who's obviously in love with you but also knows he's still got competition for your heart. Maybe it was best that he left because obviously, you're not ready to move on."

"Why did he have to die?" I sobbed. "He never saw our beautiful Madison…it's so unfair."

"Yes, life can be pretty crappy but you also have to remember those beautiful children who are depending on you to give them happy and full lives. Gage misses his daddy but he also needs his mommy to guide him and show him that everything's going to be okay. Madison will just have to find out how wonderful her daddy was from you. You can't keep Rusty from them but instead should share great stories about how much he loved all of you."

I sniffled and wiped my eyes with a tissue. "I guess I'm not the first person this has happened to and I know I won't be the last."

"I think you should get some counseling. You've had so much trauma in your life and you really need somewhere safe to spill out your feelings and also have a trained professional to help you deal with everything."

I sighed and lay back on the pillows of my bed. "You're right. I'm not dealing with this at all. I've been going through the motions and not facing the fact that Rusty's gone and I'm a widow in my twenties with two children to raise."

"You have been incredibly strong and the fact that you've held it together this long is so amazing. Rusty would want you to be happy and one day, you'll find that happiness."

"Jolene, thank you for talking with me. I know you're crazy busy with your new clients but it really means a lot."

"We're friends and that's what friends do. You are a beautiful, talented woman who is stronger than she knows. When you get back to Charlotte, I'll help you find someone to help you get yourself back together."

"I'll be back in a couple of days and I'll call you then, okay?"

"You got it. Please take care of yourself. You mean so much to so many."

We said our goodbyes then I quickly checked my phone to see if by chance I'd missed a call or text from Mason but there was nothing.

I dragged myself up from the bed and checked the time. I had an interview with a local news station scheduled in just a couple of hours so I jumped in the shower and put myself together.

When I came out of my room, I overheard Joey on the phone.

"Hey, babe, I was just thinking about you and wanted to tell you that I love you," he said in a hushed voice.

I stopped and started to back up to give him privacy but froze when I heard what he said next.

"Well, Ryder assigned him to someone else. He insisted on being taken off this assignment and he's with some senator's son who's apparently being threatened or something. I don't think I'm permanent, just a fill-in until we get back."

He paused to listen and then continued, "I really don't know what happened but when I got here, he'd already packed and hauled ass out the door to the airport. His flight wasn't for a few hours but he went anyway and slept in the terminal."

Again a pause. "Yeah, he looked pretty devastated. I don't know what went down here but it messed him up."

The more he said, the more my guts twisted into knots. Mason fled *because of me*, he was devastated *because of me*. It was all my fault and I felt sick about it. As quietly as I could, I backed up to my room and eased my door closed. I gave him a few minutes then noisily opened the door. I heard him say, "Bye, baby," as he hung up the phone.

As I walked in, he turned and smiled a sad smile. "Ms. Charles. Your car is waiting downstairs."

I grabbed my bag and dropped my phone into it but as I did, I felt a large envelope under my hand. I'd forgotten about the package I'd picked up from the front desk. Slipping my finger under the flap, I opened it and pulled out the contents. My eyes grew wide as I saw what was inside.

There were letters, hundreds of them, all written in pencil. Certain words were underlined in red marker and there were notes in the margins written in the red as well. Joey, seeing the confusion on my face, came to stand beside me. "Is everything okay?" he asked with concern.

I dropped onto the closest chair and began to read the letter addressed: *TO THE WHORE*.

YOU ARE A HORRIBLE PERSON! I LOVED RUSTY AND YOU KILLED HIM! I WAS TALKING TO THE PRESIDENT THE OTHER DAY WHEN WE WERE HAVING BREAKFAST AND HE AGREED WITH ME THAT YOU CAUSED HIS DEATH. AT FIRST I THOUGHT IT WAS A POLICE CONSPIRACY BECAUSE THEY ARE WATCHING ME ALL THE TIME, BUT THEN MY MOTHER CAME TO ME IN A DREAM AND TOLD ME THAT IT WAS YOU! SHE CAN SEE THINGS BECAUSE SHE LIVES IN HEAVEN AND HAS HER EYES ON YOU!

I MET RUSTY AT A RACE AND HE TOLD ME THAT HE LOVED ME AND WANTED ME TO HAVE HIS CHILDREN BUT THEN YOU KEPT HIM AND MY CHILDREN FROM ME! I CAN'T HAVE RUSTY BUT I CAN STILL HAVE MY CHILDREN! I CAME TO CALIFORNIA TO TAKE THEM HOME WITH ME BUT THEN YOU CAME HERE WITH YOUR LOVER INSTEAD. TRUST ME, I'LL GET THEM SOON ENOUGH. I'LL BE WAITING FOR THE PERFECT

TIME TO BRING THEM <u>HOME</u> TO ME. <u>DON'T</u> CALL THE POLICE BECAUSE <u>I'LL KNOW</u>!

M.

I felt tears falling down my cheeks as I read the letter again. Certain words were underlined more than once, especially the part about the children. I threw down the letter and ran to my bathroom where I threw myself to my knees and retched into the toilet. Faintly, I could hear Joey talking on the phone and assumed he was informing Ryder about the letters. Wiping my clammy face with a towel, I made my way back out to the living area.

"Yeah man, there are hundreds of the same letter, all written in pencil and underlined the exact same way. Someone had a LOT of time on their hands." He dropped his voice when he saw me enter the room. "Yes, sir. I'll fax this over to you right away."

I ran some cold water into a glass and leaned against the counter. "Joey, I need you to cancel the rest of my interviews. I also need to call my mom…I want to get home now!"

He nodded. "Already done. I contacted Ms. Rafe and she's on that now and Ryder is contacting the security detail with your mother and Mrs. Jamison. He thinks it's best not to alarm her or the children."

I sighed. "He's right. I don't need her to freak out." Taking a deep swallow of the icy cold water, I felt it rush down my throat causing goose bumps on my arms. When it hit my stomach, it tightened causing me to have a horrible cramp. "Joey, get us out of here."

Joey sprang into action taking care of our traveling arrangements as I ran into my room to try to pack as quickly as possible. I looked at all the clothes I'd brought and didn't even care if I ever saw them again. All I could think about was getting home as soon as possible. I'd had this envelope for a while so this person could be at my house right now stealing my kids!

Joey knocked on the door. "Ms. Charles, I have you booked on a flight that's leaving as soon as we can get to the airport and a car is waiting for us downstairs. I've arranged to have your clothes shipped to you so just grab what's essential and we're out of here."

Relief flooded over me and tears welled in my eyes. "Thank you so much," I said softly as I tucked a few things into my carry-on bag.

Within moments, we were rushing downstairs to the back of the building where the car was waiting. As I climbed into the back of the limo, out of the corner of my eye, I caught a glimpse of the same thin man I'd seen at the premiere. He was partially obscured by a large brown dumpster but I was almost positive it was him. As Joey climbed into the car, I grabbed his shoulder. "There's someone in the alley watching us," I said as calmly as I could despite the intense rush of adrenaline.

He spun around in the seat to see where I was pointing but when I looked back, the man was gone. He frowned. "Are you sure there was someone there?"

I nodded as my eyes scanned the alley for any sign of the man. "I recognized him, he was at the premiere." My heart was racing and my hands were icy and trembling. I tried to swallow but my mouth had gone dry and I couldn't catch my breath.

Joey started to get out of the car but I shook my head. "Let's just go!" He nodded, got back in and called Ryder as we sped away.

"Hey, Boss. We've got a critical threat. As soon as we get to the airport, I'll get the papers faxed to you. We're on the move and our ETA to the airport will be twenty minutes. Do you have the team over at the primary location?"

Unbuckling my seatbelt, I scooted forward to lean over the seat. "Are my babies okay?" I whispered.

He nodded and continued to talk to Ryder. "Yes, sir. She recognized someone who'd been at the premiere." His voice dropped and he turned away from me. "Sir, you may need to get Mason back on this. He could have seen this guy and could give us a heads up."

Taking a deep breath, I dropped back against the seat. Why had I screwed everything up? I closed my eyes tightly to try to stop the tears from escaping. Mason was gone and probably wanted nothing more to do with me. Joey ended his call as we pulled into the airport but we didn't head to the main terminal. Instead, we pulled through a gate that indicated a private terminal. Joey turned around and seeing my confusion explained. "Ryder made arrangements for a private jet. It'll get you home faster."

I sighed with relief. I had been dreading the thought of waiting any longer to get home. The driver parked the car next to the plane, which already had the engines running. Joey jumped from the car and began to open my door but I had it already halfway open. "I've got this," I said pulling my bag out with me.

We quickly boarded and within just a few minutes were taxiing down the runway and joined the line of aircraft waiting for clearance to take off. My phone rang and I saw it was my mom. Joey nodded that it was okay to answer and when I heard her voice, I could tell everything was okay. I kept my voice calm as I asked about the kids and explained that the trip had been cut short and that we were headed home. She told me that we had some new security people and that they were really nice. She also asked how Mason was.

"Well, Mom...he isn't with me."

"What? What's wrong? Is he okay?"

"He left. It's a long story. Joey's with me now."

She was silent for a moment then said, "Well, when you get back, you can tell me all about it."

"Sure. I'll do that…and Mom? Please do everything the security people tell you to do."

"Okay, I'll see you soon, sweetie. Love you."

The plane began to take off and within moments, we were climbing into the blue California sky headed back home to North Carolina.

I tried to take a nap but couldn't relax. I kept thinking of the letters and the creepy guy in the alleyway. I'd already been mentally beating myself up over going on this trip to begin with because I had to be away from the children, and, of course, that brought me back to Mason.

I gazed out the window at the clouds below and thought about the night we'd spent together. He'd been so gentle and loving and in my heart, I knew he had more feelings for me than he was letting show. I wasn't a conquest for him, instead I felt he treated me with more tenderness to show me that his feelings were genuine. He'd shown me the utmost respect and care yet all I could feel at the time was my own guilt and remorse. My only hope was that he may forgive me one day for everything that happened and that we could be friends again.

Chapter 11

Mason

I'd just pulled into the campus of UNC-Charlotte with my new assignment, Aaron, when my phone rang. He glared at me with contempt since he was completely disgusted that he had to have a "babysitter", as he put it.

"Let me get this and I'll walk you to class." I was met by silence and more stink-eye. He huffed and crossed his arms then began staring at the very expensive watch on his wrist. I knew he had plenty of time to get to class so I ignored the tantrum and answered. "What's up?"

Ryder cleared his throat. "Mason, we have a situation. I know you're a pretty observant guy so I need to pick your brain."

I nodded. "Yeah, that's what they tell me. What do you need?"

"Well, I need you to think back to when you were at the premiere with Ryanne. Do you recall seeing a thin man in the crowd wearing a baseball cap with Rusty MacNeil's car number on it?"

Instantly, I knew who he was talking about. Among the crowd of cheering fans, he'd stood out with his heavy jacket and hat. "Yeah, I remember him. What's going on?"

"Well, Ryanne's received a package and it contained over a hundred copies of one threatening letter. The writer of the letter targeted the kids. We're having the police look the letters over now but it was hand delivered to the hotel so no postmark."

My heart began to race. "Is she okay? Are the kids okay?"

"Yes, Joey's headed back with Ryanne on a private jet and I've got Darryl and Seth over at the house with her mom and the kids."

"Thank God." I glanced over at Aaron, who was fidgeting in his seat, still looking at his watch. "Look, I'll stop by the office once I get Mr. Fleming safely to his house this afternoon. Please keep me updated."

"Will do. Mason, I know how you feel and we're doing everything we can to make sure they're safe."

"Thanks. I really appreciate it." I hung up then unlocked the doors. "Let's get you to class."

He pouted. "This is ridiculous. I don't understand why you have to be with me all day. My mom is treating me like I'm a baby."

Trying to keep my voice even and not grit my teeth, I said, "Sir, I have been contracted to protect you. You may not feel that you're in danger but your mother does and she's paying the bill. If something happens to you, I have to answer for it. If you cooperate, this will be painless for the both of us."

He stared at me, his bottom lip still protruding. "Fine! I'll go along with this but I am not happy about it!"

I jumped out of the car, quickly scanned the area and then opened his door. He nervously emerged and I knew that despite his protests, he really was afraid that someone was going to get him. We walked into the lecture hall and after I had him tucked safely in class, I found a bench nearby to sit on. I pulled out my phone and went back through the messages I'd received from Ryanne after I left.

Looking back over them, I could see the confusion and the hurt she was feeling and I felt a huge stab of guilt about how I'd handled things. Leaving the way I did without a word was probably the worst way but I'd been trying to make things easier on her. Turns out, I was wrong. Unfortunately, I'd shown my weakness by sleeping with her and crossing that professional line with a client. I'd allowed myself to become a part of her world when I was supposed to be protecting it. She was off-limits and like a fool, I let myself think I'd be worthy of her love. She was still in love with her husband and probably always would be.

I should have said no that night she showed up at my door. I should have told her it would only make things complicated but instead, I took her into my bed without concern for the consequences. For both of our sakes, I resolved to keep myself as far away from Ryanne Charles as possible. I vowed to help Ryder and the team to keep her and the children safe but I'd have to do it indirectly. I had a new assignment and despite wanting to choke the life out him, Aaron deserved my full professional protection.

Students began to stream out of Aaron's class so I walked over to the door to wait for him to come out. The number of students dwindled and still no Aaron. I stuck my head in the door and saw the professor wiping down the white board while a couple of students feverishly typed their notes on their laptops. Aaron was nowhere to be found. I walked over to the professor and cleared my throat. He spun around and as I towered over him by at least a foot, he stepped back nervously.

"M-may I help you?" he stammered.

"Yes, did Aaron Fleming attend this class?"

He stepped over to his notebook, drew his index finger down the list of students and shook his head no. "I thought I saw him before class started but when I took attendance, he didn't answer."

I looked around the classroom and saw a side door leading out into the large courtyard. Damn that kid. He'd slipped away. "Thank you for your time," I said as I quickly made my way across the classroom to the exit door. When I opened it, I could see hundreds of students making their way to their next classes or sitting in the grassy areas reading or having lunch. He had an hour head start. I'd never find him this way. I called his mother and explained that he'd given me the slip.

She sounded distressed. "That boy! He has no sense! He doesn't have a clue what someone could do to him just because he's my child. I need you to find him as soon as possible, Mr. Leffler. If anything happens to my son, I'll never forgive you."

"Yes, ma'am. I'll do my best." I hung up the phone and stood with my hands on my hips trying to think where I would go if I was in his shoes. I ran back to the car, opened my trunk, and pulled out the folder. I looked down the list of known contacts and saw he had a girlfriend. Bingo! Any man feeling emasculated by his mother, would no doubt go to his girlfriend to get his ego pumped back up. I jumped into the car and headed to the address I had in the file. I ran up the steps and knocked on the door. I saw the curtain at the window move and the sound of footsteps inside. A moment later, the door cracked and a young brunette woman stuck her head out the door.

"Can I help you?" she asked, slightly out of breath.

"Yes, are you Trish Voss?" I knew it was her because I had a photo but I asked anyway.

She nodded slowly. "Yes, that's me. What can I do for you?"

"I'm looking for Aaron Fleming. Have you seen him?"

She glanced back nervously and then shook her head. "Nope, haven't seen him. Are you a cop or something?"

I smiled. "No, I'm his protection. You see, someone has threatened him and anyone who is with him is in danger as well."

Her eyes grew wide. "D-danger? What kind of danger?"

"Well, the person who's threatened him may try to hurt the people he cares about to get to him."

She took a step back pulling the door open. "He's in the bedroom."

"Thank you for your cooperation," I said as I stepped past her into the apartment. I located the only bedroom and quickly found Aaron hiding in the closet under a pile of dirty laundry. Trisha followed me into the room and immediately he began to yell at her.

"Why'd you tell him? He's working for my mother," he shrieked as I held out my hand to help him up from the floor. He ignored my hand while still glaring at Trisha.

"Aaron, you didn't tell me someone threatened you. You told me your mom was just being overprotective." She walked over to lean against the door frame. "You need to do what this man says so he can keep you safe."

He bowed his head and stared at the floor. "You're right. But Trisha, he's making me feel like a prisoner," he whined again.

She walked over and placed her hand on his cheek. "I want you safe, I love you."

He turned his face to her hand and kissed her palm. "I love you too."

I clenched my jaw watching this play out in front of me. This could have been Ryanne and I...

Aaron turned to me and sighed. "I'm sorry I left like I did."

I shrugged. "It's your choice to leave but it's my obligation to follow you."

He stared at me for a moment then smiled. "I guess you're right. It doesn't feel as crazy when you say it that way."

I put my hand on his shoulder. "Sir, when we have the person who's threatening you, you won't need me anymore and you can go back to your life."

Trisha walked over and took his hand. "Aaron, I'm sure they'll figure it all out soon."

He nodded and kissed her lightly on the lips. "I'll call you later. Sorry I put you in the middle of all this."

She smiled. "It's okay. You'll just owe me a big dinner when it's over."

We walked down to the car and climbed in. "Mr. Leffler, thanks for not making things weird in there. My mom would've totally made a scene."

"No problem. Now, let's get you back to school." I dropped him back off at his next class and since there were extra seats, I sat in the back. The class had laptops on the desks so I did some research while the professor lectured to the students.

Ryder had told me that the letters that were written to Ryanne were in pencil with certain words underlined in red. Using my law enforcement connections, I had access to files of known criminals who had used that same method to threaten their victims. I got a hit but it wasn't what I expected. The file revealed an elderly woman who had been in and out of jail for threatening several different celebrities and in each case, she used letters written exactly the same way. I kept searching, hoping to turn up someone with a history of harassing public figures who matched the description of the thin man I'd seen at the premiere but had no luck. I was jotting down the information I did manage to get just as the class finished. Aaron came right up to me and waited patiently for me to escort him to his final class of the day. The day was dragging along and it was frustrating not knowing what was happening with Ryanne. I mentally kicked myself for leaving when I did.

When we arrived at Aaron's final class, we found out it had been canceled. According to the note on the door, his professor had come down with a bad case of food poisoning. I breathed a sigh of relief knowing that I was almost free to head back to the office to check on Ryanne. My assignment was to protect Aaron while he was at school since when he was at home, the senator had her own protection and they would watch out for him while he was there. Before I left the house, I made him promise me that he'd stay close to home until we figured out who was making the threats against him.

I drove out of the opulent neighborhood that the Fleming's called home, dropped him off, then headed downtown to the office. Ryder and I ended up parking at the same time and we walked into the building together.

"So, what's the latest on the Fleming case," Ryder asked as he flipped through a large stack of papers.

"Well, everything went smoothly at the college today and I've done some preliminary checking on where the email threats originated from. I've got a friend in the Charlotte PD checking with their Internet Forensics department to see if we can get an IP address of the subject."

He continued to scan the papers as he nodded. "So, no issues then." I hesitated for a moment and he glanced over at me. "What's up, Mason?"

"Well, he got away from me today and headed to his girlfriend's house. I tracked him down and once I made it clear that his ditching me wasn't an option, he went willingly back to school."

Ryder tucked the papers under his arm and punched the elevator button. "The little rich kid managed to shake you? That's pretty funny," he said with a chuckle.

I folded my arms and stared at the numbers over the door and counted down the floors as the elevator dropped to the lobby. When I didn't respond, he patted me on the shoulder. "Man, I know what's on your mind and when we get to the office, I'll give you the latest information. She's okay and that's all that matters right now."

I sighed with relief. "Thanks for the update. I just can't stand not knowing what's going on."

We stepped into the elevator and headed up to our floor. "Mason, Joey's with her and they're back at her house. I got a private jet to pick them up so she didn't have to wait any longer to get back."

She was back. I clenched my fists to try to get myself calmed down. All I wanted to do was drive over there and take her in my arms but I couldn't...not now. Instead, I forced myself to think of her just as a client, no matter how impossible that might be.

We arrived at our floor and as we walked to the office, Jolene and her sister Olivia came out of their suite. She smiled at Ryder and rushed over to kiss him. "Hey, baby! Are you going to be coming home with me tonight?" she asked with a pout.

He pulled her into his arms and kissed her forehead. "No, I'm afraid I'll be late tonight. I've got several things to finish up before I can head home."

She frowned. "Well, then I guess I'll just have to go on a dinner date with Liv."

Olivia smiled at Ryder. "I promise I'll take good care of her. Since Joey's gone, I'm all by my lonesome."

Ryder glanced over at her. "Joey's back but he's going to be working round the clock at Ryanne's house until further notice."

Olivia's eyes flickered over to me then back to Ryder. "You mean he's going to be living there? What the heck is going on?"

Ryder pulled away from Jolene and walked over to Olivia. "Look, it's part of his job. I had to send him. We have a viable threat to her and she's in need of security and Joey's the guy. You don't know the situation and if you did, you'd understand why I had to send Joey." He looked back at me. "Mason's here because I needed him here for another assignment, one more suited to his skills."

Her shoulders sagged and she sighed. "I'm sorry. I just worry about him and now you're telling me he's in a dangerous situation. You can see where I have a right to be concerned."

Ryder pulled her into a hug. "Liv, you know I wouldn't put Joey in a situation he couldn't handle. He's got top military training and is as smart as hell. He'll be just fine. Plus, we're in constant communication so if there's any sign of trouble, I'll have backup over to him immediately."

Jolene spoke up. "So, my sister and I are going to get out of here and grab some dinner at Libretto's. Do you want me to have them deliver some pizza for you since you'll be working late?"

Ryder pulled her into his arms and gave her a soft kiss. "Baby, you take such good care of me. I'd love that. Don't forget, extra pepperoni."

She grinned and pinched his cheek. "Of course." She linked her arm through Olivia's and blew him another kiss as they headed to the elevator.

Ryder smiled as he opened the door to the office. Darryl was sitting in one of the chairs balancing a folder on his knee. He was writing notes and looked up as we came in.

"Hey, guys. I'm just finishing up my report."

Ryder clapped him on the shoulder. "How's everything with Tyson?"

He laughed. "Boss, I appreciate the job but…"

Ryder looked surprised. "There's a but?"

"It's hard to look intimidating when the guy you're protecting is over a foot taller than you," he said grinning.

Ryder shrugged. "So, he's a pro basketball player. He's skilled on the court but not in self-defense. Some of these fans get crazy and you're the last line of defense between them and him. Besides, you scare the hell out of me."

Darryl stood up towering over Ryder by at least six inches. "Me? Scare you? Dude, it's always the little guys that are dangerous. You're fast!"

Ryder grinned and strolled over to sit at his desk. "You're right, fast and wiry! That's me!"

We followed him into the office and sat in chairs across from him. Darryl leaned back in the chair and tented his fingers. "So, what's the latest on the Charles case?"

Ryder glanced quickly at me then back to Darryl. He pulled out a file folder and handed each of us a copy of the letter Ryanne had received. I quickly glanced down the page and felt prickles up and down my skin. One line stood out and it made me realize that someone was definitely watching her very closely. *I CAME TO CALIFORNIA TO TAKE THEM HOME WITH ME BUT THEN YOU CAME HERE WITH YOUR LOVER INSTEAD.* Whoever had written this obviously thought Ryanne and I were lovers. I glanced up to find Ryder watching me closely.

Darryl continued to read and made notes in the margins of the page. I could feel myself getting more and more agitated as I thought about someone watching us together and me not noticing them as a possible threat. I cleared my throat and asked, "I know this is going to sound stupid but do you think this could be a man?"

Ryder shrugged. "At this point, anything's possible. A delusional mind can make anything seem like reality. In my gut, I'm going with a woman but I can't rule anything out. We really don't have a suspect except for the strange man that Ryanne saw lurking in the alley behind the hotel.

184

Mason, she said she saw him at the premiere. Do you remember a thin man wearing a cap with Rusty's car number on it?"

I closed my eyes and replayed that night in my head. I tried to visualize the crowd and suddenly, it came to me. The man had been standing next to a very loud woman who had been waving a picture of Ryanne along with an autograph book. I quickly made a rough sketch of both of them just to be on the safe side.

Darryl glanced over at my sketch and his eyes grew wide. "Nice work, man. If I'd have done it, we'd be looking for a couple of stick figures."

Ryder stood then walked over to stand next to me. "Well, we have at least something to go on. Darryl, can you run this over to her house and see if she thinks this is pretty close?"

I opened my mouth to volunteer to take it but then shut it quickly. No matter how much I wanted to go, she didn't want me there. I had to face the fact and stay out of her life. She needed time to heal and even though I wanted her more than anything in this world, I also needed to respect that.

Darryl reached over and slid the paper from my lap. "I'll run it over right now. While I'm there, I'll double check everything and make sure Joey's all set up."

Ryder checked his watch. "Jolene ordered some pizza and it should be here any minute. Do you want to grab some before you go?"

He shook his head. "Pizza isn't on my list. Tyson has me training with him since I'm at the gym most of the time. He's trying to make me lean."

Ryder laughed. "Okay, more for Mason and me. Call me when you get over there with an update."

As soon as Darryl closed the door, Ryder said, "I know this is hard for you. You look like you're about to jump out of your skin."

I took a deep breath and blew it out. "I'm going nuts. I want to be over there with her but I know she's better off without me in the picture."

He shook his head. "Well, I can tell you, she's very unhappy about the whole situation."

I stood and began to pace. "I think the hardest thing for me about this whole thing is that I don't know what to feel. You've probably already figured out what happened and why I had to leave." When he nodded, I continued, "I'm competing with a ghost and not just any ghost. A ghost who was perfect in every way. How do you stack up against someone like that? I'm just a divorced ex-cop who doesn't measure up to someone like Rusty MacNeil. I don't even know why I thought I could."

Ryder sat down in his chair, his eyes following me as I paced. "You're really selling yourself short, Mason. You're more than just a divorced ex-cop and you know it. In this job, you have to have a line between you and the subject or else it compromises the assignment. Sometimes, it's impossible not to cross it. That's how it was for Jolene and me. I've loved her since we were kids and when I took on the job of protecting her, I knew that it was wrong. I knew I should let someone else handle it because my feelings were going to impair my judgment but I did it anyway. I'm glad I did because when Marco kidnapped her, I knew I had to be the one to save her. She was mine. You feel that way about Ryanne and there's nothing wrong with that. You care about her and the kids. I can see it when you're with them. Whatever happened between you two in California obviously put a rift between you. Honestly, I don't think she has a clue what to do next."

I stopped and stared. "Ryder, she just needs to worry about herself and her kids and not be concerned with me. I was a diversion, plain and simple. As much as it hurts, I can harden my heart again and move on. She needs to do the same."

A knock came on the outer office door. Ryder studied me for a moment then got up and walked out of his office. I slumped back onto the chair and buried my face in my hands. My gut was in knots and I realized I was clenching my jaw tightly.

Ryder walked in and dropped a large pizza box onto his desk. "You okay?" he asked.

"I will be. Listen, I need some air. When you get an update from Darryl, could you please text me?"

"Sure. You gonna eat something?" he asked pushing the pizza box toward me.

My stomach lurched again as thoughts of someone targeting Ryanne and the kids raced through my mind. "No, I'm sorry. I've gotta go."

"I'll keep you updated. Mason, get some rest. We all need to be on top of our game."

I nodded and left. The ride in the elevator seemed endless but soon I was down on the street in the fresh air. I started walking, hoping to clear my head but all I could think about was Ryanne. I passed a couple walking on the sidewalk and I caught a whiff of her perfume. It was the same one that Ryanne wore. I was so tempted to follow them just to breathe in that sweet scent for a little while longer but I knew that wasn't an option. They'd probably feel threatened and call the cops and truthfully, I wouldn't blame them. Instead, I stopped at a bar and ordered a drink which turned into two. I stared at my reflection in the mirror above the bar and felt as if I were looking at a stranger and it sickened me.

I threw a few dollars on the bar and drove back to my apartment. As I climbed the steps, I heard a woman's voice call my name. My heart leapt and I spun around hoping to find Ryanne coming to me. To my surprise, I found my ex-wife.

Chapter 12

Ryanne

I heard the front door bell and some voices downstairs but I didn't move for fear of waking the kids. Since coming home from California, I'd been very clingy and paranoid about having them leave my sight. My mom was worried about me and told me that I needed to talk to someone but the only person I wanted to talk to was Mason.

I pulled Gage a little closer to me and kissed the top of his head. He was snoring and had his hand tucked under his cheek. He stirred slightly then went right back to snoring. Madison was sleeping in the crook of my arm, nestled between Gage and me. She'd been fussy all day and finally settled down and I knew it was because they were unfamiliar with the new man in the house. Joey was a really sweet guy and a true professional but he wasn't Mason. Gage had clung to my mom when we'd come in and he spent most of the time since we'd been home in his room playing with his toys. Madison had cried when she saw Joey and he tried to make her laugh but it was a definite no-go. Gage asked, "Where's Mason?" and I had to try to explain that he had another important job to take care of but my words rang hollow. He'd looked at me, frowned, then crossed his arms over his little chest and stormed back to his room.

My mom tried to find out what had happened but I just couldn't bear to tell her. Being back in the house I'd shared with Rusty made it even harder. His things were still in the closet. His toiletries were still on the vanity. I was surrounded by memories and it made me feel even more guilt over what had happened between Mason and me.

I closed my eyes and pictured Mason standing at the door of his bedroom and that was when I realized that there were two men downstairs talking. My heart leapt at the thought that Mason might have come back after all. I slid my arm from around Madison and eased off of the bed without disturbing them. I crept out the door and stopped at the top of the stairs. I could hear Joey talking to someone but couldn't make out the other voice. As quietly as I could, I made my way down the stairs, still trying to figure out who he was talking to. Finally, I got to the bottom and peeked around the door frame. Disappointment washed over me as I realized it was Darryl. He glanced over and saw me and smiled.

"Hey, Ms. Charles. You're just the person I need to talk to," he said walking toward me.

My face flushed with embarrassment at being seen. "Hey, Darryl, what can I do for you?" I asked trying to act nonchalant.

He handed me a piece of paper and watched me closely. I glanced down and gasped. "This is the guy!" I said, my voice cracking.

"Can you tell me how you know this man?" he asked as he glanced over at Joey with a nod.

"Yes, he was at my premiere. I know it's weird but he stood out from the crowd because he was wearing a hat with Rusty's team on it. It caught my eye and I remember getting a strange vibe from him. He wasn't cheering or calling out to me, he just stared. He was also in the alley when we left the hotel." Seeing his face made me shiver.

Darryl wrote down everything I said in a notebook. He asked me if I could add anything to the drawing but it was so spot-on that I didn't have to. "Who did this drawing?" I asked as I handed it to Joey. "It's so accurate."

"Mason did it," he said not looking up from his notes.

"Mason?" I squeaked out.

He looked up and nodded. "Yeah, Ryder has the entire team working on identifying this person."

"So, Mason knows everything that's going on?" I said softly.

"Yep, he was at the office with Ryder going over the file when I left."

I felt tears spring to my eyes and I quickly blinked them away. Mason was working the case because he was a part of the team. No doubt I'd crushed any feelings he'd ever had for me when I'd made it clear I couldn't move on. The sad part was that if anyone could have helped me do that, it was Mason. He was my friend and I felt safe with him.

"Is everything okay?" Darryl touched my arm with concern in his eyes. "You look really pale."

I nodded and faked a yawn giving me an excuse to wipe my eyes in the process. "Yeah, I'm fine, just exhausted from all of this. I'm going to go back upstairs and get some rest. If you need anything else, please let me know."

Darryl and Joey both nodded and said goodnight and I turned to head back up the stairs. As I reached the top step, I glanced over to the right to Mason's room. Well, it wasn't his anymore. Ryder had said that he'd send someone to get his things sometime soon making it final. Glancing back down over the railing, I could see Darryl and Joey making their way into the kitchen. I crept over to

Mason's room and turned the knob. As soon as I entered, I felt such a sense of loss for the two men in my life. Rusty would have a piece of my heart forever but he was gone and I was finally accepting that.

Mason had taken my broken heart and had given me hope that I could feel something again instead of the numbness I'd dealt with ever since the accident. I sat down on his bed and looked around the room. It was almost ironic that his things were just as he'd left them and so were Rusty's. I hadn't had the heart to try to box anything up, it just seemed so final. I imagined having all of his things ready to donate and him walking in the house saying, "Where are you taking all my stuff, darlin'?" But that wasn't going to happen.

On the other hand, Mason would be coming back to get his stuff and when he did, I'd lose him forever as well. I hugged myself and lay back onto the bed. Mason's cologne lingered on the bed covers and I lay my face against the soft down comforter and breathed it in. Memories of our time together came flashing back and I felt so alone and lost. Choking back tears, I jumped from the bed and ran into my bedroom.

I rushed into the bathroom and splashed cold water on my face. Dabbing my face dry, I looked around the bathroom at all of Rusty's toiletries. I rushed to my closet and pulled out an old shoebox then with one sweep, I raked all of his things into it. I peered out the bathroom door to make sure the kids were still fast asleep then I went into the closet. I pulled out a huge tote box and began to fold Rusty's clothes and placed them gently in it. Somewhere, someone would benefit from these clothes and it was time to give them a new home. Each piece of clothing held a memory for me and the effect was calming and I felt a sense of peace come over me. As I folded the shirt from our first date, I smiled thinking of how nervous we'd both been and how quickly that had passed. We'd spent hours talking and ended up sitting in his convertible watching the sun rise. I knew then I was going to marry him one day.

I ran my hands through the closet and found the blazer he'd worn when he proposed. He'd made an elaborate plan to propose on the beach at sunset but the weather hadn't cooperated and a storm had come up throwing off his entire scheme. We'd had to run to get out of the downpour and ended up in the doorway of an ice cream parlor. With our hair dripping wet and water running down our cheeks, he'd touched my face gently then dropped to one knee right there and asked me to marry him. I remember a cheer going up when I nodded and said yes and I looked around to find a crowd pressed against the window watching our every move. It was perfect.

The tuxedo he'd worn to our wedding was tucked into the back of the closet and I as I pulled it out, I ran my hands over the silky material and the memory of our first dance and the wedding came to mind. He'd surprised me and had his friend Lucas sing for us as we danced and I remembered laughing and crying at the same time. It had been a magical night. Absently, I ran my hands through the pockets and I found a piece of paper tucked into the breast pocket. I unfolded it and held it close to the light. It was his vows, written in his own handwriting and I again found a wave of peace flow over me. He'd promised to love me for as long as he lived and I'd done the same. It was a promise I would keep and the memories would help me do just that. After safely tucking the vows into my jewelry box, I put the special clothes into a box for the kids to have one day and then packed up the other things to donate to a person in need, anonymously, of course. I didn't want his things to end up in a bidding war on some celebrity memorabilia website, I wanted someone to have a warm jacket or new shoes. It had been several hours and I'd packed up pretty much everything.

Suddenly, I felt the need to talk to Mason. Not to ask him to come back, but to just talk to him as a friend. I checked the time and it was almost nine. He'd probably finished his meeting with Ryder and was headed home for the night. I got dressed in some yoga pants and a sweatshirt, threw my hair up in a clip and then knocked on my mom's door. She opened it with a confused look on her face. "What's wrong, sweetie?"

"Mom, I need to talk to Mason. Can you keep an eye on the kids for a little while?"

She glanced over at my bedroom where the kids were sprawled across my bed. "Well, sure but you're not going alone are you? You're going to take Joey with you, right?"

Crap. I hadn't thought about that. I was under protection and couldn't just waltz out on my own. Thinking quickly I said, "Sure, he's going with me. I won't be long. You can go in my room and watch television, if you want."

She smiled and nodded. "Okay, just don't be late." She kissed me on the cheek and went into my room and shut the door. I leaned over the railing and saw that Darryl had left and Joey was sitting in the den munching on a sandwich watching a movie. As quietly as I could, I made my way downstairs and moved quickly into the kitchen then out the back door. I ran across the lawn and around the tree line to the extra garage where we had Rusty's convertible mustang parked. Since we'd had Gage, we'd driven an SUV when we'd gone out as a family. The convertible was something Rusty liked to tinker on and polish when he had time. I slid the garage door up and climbed in. Praying it would start, I turned the key. It fired up on the first try and I eased it out of the garage, slid the door back down and left, careful not to turn on the lights until I was past the house and Joey's watchful eye. Once I cleared the view of the house, I eased up to the gate and it opened and I was off. Flipping the switch for the roof, it folded back and tucked itself into the back of the car. The wind in my hair was invigorating and I actually felt alive for the first time in a while. I glanced down at the envelope I'd snagged from Mason's room with his address on it and turned into the apartment complex. I scanned the buildings for numbers and found the one I was looking for. Pulling into an empty space, I jumped out of the car and jogged toward the building but stopped when I heard Mason's voice.

"Hello, Kristin," he was saying.

The woman laughed. "Is that any way to greet your *wife*?"

"You're *not* my wife," he snapped.

I tucked myself under the staircase they were standing on and tried to listen over my heartbeat roaring in my ears.

"Where's Tom?"

She let out a shrill laugh. "Tom? Oh, he found a younger version of me. We've been divorced about a year now."

He chuckled. "Well, I guess karma really is a bitch."

She took a step closer to him. "I guess I deserve that. Don't you remember how we were when we first met? Eating mac n' cheese for dinner by candlelight because we couldn't afford the electric? I've had a lot of time to remember and it made me realize that I let the best man I've ever known get away."

"Kristin, don't. There isn't any future for us. We're history."

She climbed another step and I noticed he hadn't moved away. "Mason, we were so good together and I was happy until you started working all those late hours. What was I supposed to do? Someone paid me some attention and I fell for it. I was stupid and it shouldn't have happened."

"How many men were there, Kristin? I know Tom wasn't the first."

She sighed. "I'll admit he wasn't the first but Mason, I want you to be the last. I want to grow old with you and if God's willing, I want to have a baby with you. I need you, baby."

Mason's silence was like a knife to my gut. I wanted to scream at him to run away from her but I was frozen in place. Finally, he said, "Look, I think you need to leave." Under the stairs, I was trying desperately not to make a sound but I did a little fist pump when he said that.

Kristin wasn't going to give up that easily. "No, Mason. I want to be with you. I want you to make love to me like you used to. We were so good together and I screwed it up. Can't you give me another chance? Is there someone else? Have I lost you?"

He didn't speak for a moment then I heard him take a step toward her. My heart sank as I heard him say, "There's no one else."

Tears burned my eyes and I spun to try to run blindly back to my car. I tripped over a hedge but managed to get in the driver's seat and with a trembling hand, cranked the car. The engine roared to life and as I turned the headlights on, I could see Mason walking toward the car shielding his eyes from the glare. I threw the car in reverse then slammed it into drive and spun out of the parking lot. A few minutes down the road, I had to pull over to catch my breath. I was having a full-blown panic attack and I couldn't breathe. I pulled into the parking lot of a motel and tried to collect myself. I concentrated on slowing my breathing and that eased the horrible pounding in my head. I felt so stupid for even thinking that this was a good idea and after hearing what I did, I knew that he had no feelings left for me.

Chapter 13

Mason

The last person I wanted to see was standing only three feet from me. My head was already splitting from the day I'd had and now I had my ex-wife literally at my feet. Kristin had always been a beautiful woman. Tall, brunette and olive skinned, she had used her looks to get me and unfortunately, she hadn't stopped there. After our divorce, I found out that she'd had several affairs including one with my captain. Seeing her now, I felt nothing but disgust at the person I knew was inside the pretty exterior.

Right away, she began her pitch, which I expected. Why else would she be in North Carolina except to try to sink her claws back into me. When she told me Tom had left her for a younger woman, I couldn't help but laugh. She seemed eager to see me but I knew she had some motive, some reason for being here besides her undying love for me. I wanted her to leave but she kept moving closer until she was standing one step below me. Suddenly, I caught a whiff of perfume and it shook me for a moment. It was the same fragrance that Ryanne wore. Fighting back my feelings, when she asked if I had someone, I said no to convince myself that I needed to be moving on. A moment later, I heard someone come from underneath the stairs and run across the parking lot. Instantly, my guard went up and I pushed Kristin to the side as I ran down the stairs. Whoever it was had made it to their car and their bright headlights blinded me from getting a good look at them. The whole thing seemed really suspicious and I was tempted to jump in my car and follow but I also remembered I'd had a couple of drinks and with my luck, I'd get stopped before I even hit the main road and cops aren't so forgiving of ex-cops who've had a few.

I turned back around and ran right into Kristin, who took the opportunity to press herself tightly against me. "Mason," she purred. "Please don't make me go home alone tonight. I want you." She wrapped her arms tightly around my waist and kissed the bare skin of my throat. I reached down and pulled her arms from around me and firmly pushed her away.

"Go home, Kristin. I don't want you. I don't need you, I don't need anyone."

Her bottom lip began to quiver and tears welled in her eyes. "I can't believe I loved you. You're so cold and cruel."

I shook my head and shrugged. "You get what you give. I have a heart and will be more than willing to give it to someone who won't tear it apart like you did. You chose to warm another man's bed and now you'll sleep alone."

I brushed by her and climbed the steps, two at a time, leaving her standing there. Once inside the apartment, my mind went back to the person who was obviously spying on me. As a precaution, I texted Joey to make sure Ryanne was okay and he texted back that everything was fine.

The whole day had rattled me so I grabbed a beer before dropping onto the couch to catch up on the news.

I woke up the next morning on the couch with the beer bottle unopened on the table. The television was still on and the reporter was giving the traffic report for the early morning commuters. I crawled off of the couch and felt a twinge in my back from laying wrong but managed to get in the shower and felt a little better for it. I was just about to leave to meet Aaron when I got a call from Ryder.

"Hey, Mason. Have you left yet?"

"No, I was just heading out. What's up?"

"Senator Fleming called this morning. The FBI tracked down the person who was making the threats and arrested them this morning. It turns out it was his girlfriend Trish Voss. It seems she was dating a guy who should have gotten a scholarship but lost out to Aaron. She and the boyfriend cooked up an elaborate plot to get him to quit school. She'd placed herself in Aaron's hangouts and conned him into thinking everything was by chance. She'd already done research on the poor kid and knew all of his likes and dislikes which she used to her advantage. Aaron's obviously devastated but at least he's safe. The senator was very pleased with how well you worked with him and sent us a substantial bonus for our brief but excellent work. I'll cut you a check and have it waiting for you when you come in. Hang on a sec. I'm getting a call from Joey."

He put me on hold and while I waited, I made myself some very strong coffee to try to shake the funk of last night. A moment later, he came back on the phone.

"Mason, we've got a problem." His voice was filled with concern.

"What's up?" I felt the hair stand up on the back of my neck.

"Ryanne's missing."

"WHAT? How is that possible? Joey said everything was okay last night!" I grabbed my keys and headed out the door.

"Joey just called."

I jumped in my car and backed out, my tires squealing on the asphalt as I kicked it into drive. "So, when's the last time he saw her?"

"He said that when he went to bed, her bedroom door was closed so he assumed she was in there. This morning, when he got up, he met her mom coming out of her room and she told him that she'd gone to see you last night around nine."

My throat tightened and I felt my heart skip a beat. "She came to see me? I haven't seen her!" I realized I was shouting so I took a deep breath and tried to calm myself to stay rational. "Dammit, that's almost ten hours ago!"

"Mason, calm down. I know you're freaking out, I am too. Get to Ryanne's as soon as you can."

I hung up the phone then dialed her number. It went straight to voicemail so I threw my phone onto the seat and gripped the steering wheel tightly. Weaving through traffic, I replayed last night in my head. Had Ryanne been the one under the stairs? I tried to remember exactly what I'd said to Kristin but my mind was a jumble of thoughts.

I rolled up into the driveway at her house and hit the security key. The gate opened excruciatingly slow but finally it was wide enough to get through and I sped into the courtyard. Slamming the car into park, I jumped out and jogged toward the house. The front door opened and Joey stepped out onto the steps.

"Mason, Ryder told me to stop you here until you calm down. The kids are inside and we don't want to scare the hell out of them," he said holding up his hands to slow my progress.

I stopped reluctantly but I totally understood. I didn't need to blast into the house and make a bad situation worse.

"So, how the hell did she get away?" I asked looking over at the SUV still parked in front of the house.

Joey shook his head and shrugged. "We haven't figured that out yet. We don't think she would've left on foot. It's too far to town."

I spun around, my eyes searching the area. "Is the boat still here?" I started walking toward the lake to check the pier.

"Yeah, we already checked that. That was the first place I checked after I saw the truck was here.

"Damn, where is she?" I scrubbed my face with my hand and paced trying to get my thoughts together. "Think, Mason, think."

Joey clapped me on the back. "Mason, we'll find her.

Desperately, I said, "We have to."

Ryder pulled into the yard and walked over to join us. "So, what's the latest?"

Joey filled him in while I walked around looking for any signs of a direction she might have gone in. I walked down to the pier to satisfy myself that the boat was still there and then turned back toward the house. Out of the corner of my eye, I saw the faint outline of a building behind the underbrush in the woods. I headed toward it and when I got closer, I could see it was a metal garage. The padlock was hanging open on the front lip of the door so I slid the door up. The garage was empty. There had been a car in here recently because I could still smell exhaust lingering inside.

"Joey! Ryder!" I called out.

Joey and Ryder came running around the edge of the woods and stopped and stared. "I never knew this was here!" Joey said in disbelief.

"We need to find out what was parked in here. Then we'll have a car to look for," I said as I headed back to the house with Ryder and Joey in tow.

We entered the house and as soon as we did, I felt tiny arms wrap around my legs.

"Mason!" Gage squealed. "I missed you!"

I placed my hand on his head and ruffled his hair as I tried to keep my composure. "Hey, buddy. I've missed you too!"

Cara came into the foyer carrying Madison, who was giggling and waving her hands in the air. Cara was smiling until she noticed Ryanne wasn't with me. She frowned then her eyes grew wide. "Is everything okay?" she asked with a shaky voice.

Looking down at Gage, I said as calmly as possible, "It will be."

She nodded slowly. "I trust you, Mason. Whatever's going on, I know you're going to make sure of that."

Joey took her by the arm. "Cara, let me fill you in on what we know." He escorted her to the living room leaving Gage with me.

"Mason, are you gonna stay with me?" he asked as he tugged on my pant leg.

I knelt down in front of him and put my hands on his tiny shoulders. "I can't stay right now but hopefully I'll be back soon, okay?"

He nodded and smiled. "Okay. Mommy misses you too. I think she's still sleeping."

Cara came into the foyer and took Gage by the hand. "Sweetie, let's go play in your room." She gave me a knowing look and a weak smile.

After they left, I called my friend Mike in the Charlotte PD and had him do a search on registrations for any cars that Rusty owned. He pulled up the record and found that the car was a rare 1966 mustang in vintage burgundy. While I was on the phone, he found a picture of it from a car show that Rusty had entered, so he texted it to me and I forwarded it to Ryder, Joey and Darryl.

Mike also told me, as a favor to me, since they didn't have an official missing persons report, that they'd put out an alert for the car to the local officers and if anyone spotted it, they'd call me immediately.

As I hung up the phone, Cara came up behind me. "Mason, I don't know what happened between you two but I think you need to see something." She led me up the stairs to Ryanne's room and into the massive closet off of the bathroom. "She's been so depressed since she came home and I thought it was because of Rusty but…" She pointed to several boxes stacked in the closet. I pulled back the lid and saw that they were filled with her husband's things. "I think she is trying to move on but she's scared."

I swallowed hard thinking of Ryanne surrounded by all of these memories. It had to have been unbelievably painful to pack these things up. "We…we got too close," I said huskily.

She nodded. "Mason, you think you're hiding your feelings but they were pretty obvious to me. You love her and you love those kids. There's nothing wrong with that."

I turned to face her. "I needed to respect this," I said gesturing toward the symbols of the life and history she'd had with her husband.

She frowned and shook her head. "Mason, she will always love him but she deserves the love and respect that you can give her. There's nothing wrong with finding love again, people do it all the time. She wouldn't be replacing him with you, she'd be making a new life. Can you picture your life without her? Can you leave her behind?"

I felt tears well in my eyes at the thought of losing her. "No, I can't. My heart belongs to her and always will...if she wants it."

She placed her hand on my arm. "Then you need to find her and bring her back home."

Wiping my eyes with the sleeve of my jacket, I nodded. "I'll find her or die trying. Thank you, Cara."

She smiled sadly. "You're a good man. Now, go."

Chapter 14

Ryanne

They say you should always follow your gut instincts and looking back, I should have done that exact thing. When I'd pulled off the road to calm my panic attack, I never noticed the car that pulled in behind me. When I wiped my eyes and looked up in the mirror, I saw a flashing blue light. In my side mirror, I could see someone climb from the car and so I dug in the console for the registration. As I turned to speak to the officer, I was blinded by the beam of a flashlight.

"Ma'am is everything okay?" It was a female's voice.

Holding up my license and registration, I answered, "Yes, I'm sorry. I pulled over because I was upset."

The officer took the paper from my hand, still keeping the light shining directly into my eyes. "Ma'am, is your name Ryanne Charles MacNeil?"

I nodded. "Yes, it is."

"Could you please step out of the car?"

Puzzled, I unbuckled my seatbelt and climbed from the car. "Is there a problem?" I had asked.

"Please turn around," the officer ordered.

I turned around and suddenly felt a sharp blow to the back of my head. As I slid down to the ground, the world went black.

When I opened my eyes, I found myself laying on a faded flowery couch. My head was pounding and I tried to reach up to touch my head but quickly realized my wrists were bound together. Groaning, I rolled over and tried to focus my eyes. When I did, I could see a woman sitting in a chair directly across from me. She was an older woman, but it was hard to estimate her age. She was wearing a heavy winter sweater despite it being the middle of summer. Her graying hair was pulled back into a ponytail and she had a bell hanging around her neck on a red string. She was leaning forward studying me and smiled when I looked at her.

"It's 'bout time you woke up. I thought I'd killed ya."

My mind was so foggy but when she said that, everything came rushing back to me. "Did you hit me?" I managed to gasp, despite my dry mouth.

She sat back and laughed. "Hit you? Nah that was a love tap. If I'd really hit ya, you *would* be dead."

I stared at her in disbelief. "Why would you do that?"

She rubbed her chin with her fingers as she studied me. "Well, I had to get you to come with me and I doubt ya would have done it willingly."

"But why?" I whispered.

She laughed and I noticed she had only a few teeth and those were brown with rot. "Because you need to be punished. You kept me from Rusty and now he's gone."

She shook her finger at me. "You will know how much I've suffered by the time I'm through with you."

I swallowed hard. "I'm sorry if I did anything to hurt you," I said softly, trying not to anger her.

She picked up a soda can and spit into it. Again she grinned showing me those teeth that were now covered in what I could only assume was tobacco juice. "It's okay, sweetie. Even though Rusty's gone, I can still have a piece of him. I'll just raise his children, like he wanted me to," she said it so matter of fact that it gave me a shiver down my spine. She stood, walked over to a broken bookcase and picked up a picture in a frame. She carried it over to me and held it directly in front of my face. In the picture, I could see Rusty standing next to this woman with his arm around her. She had a pit pass around her neck and was decked out from head to toe in Rusty's team gear. She had her index finger pointed up in the air matching Rusty's, obviously indicating he was number one. She looked at the picture and her hard expression softened. "He asked me my name and when I told him, he said it so pretty-like that I knew he was in love with me. I asked him about his young-un and he told me all about him. He said he'd love to have babies with me and they'd be as cute as bugs but I'm too old for that so I'll just have to make due with yours. I know you have a girl now so I'll take 'em both."

My stomach rolled at the thought of this woman being anywhere near my children. I had to swallow back the bile that rose into my throat. "Ma'am," I managed to say as calmly as I could. "I'm sure you were mistaken. Rusty and I were very happily married."

Anger flashed in her eyes. "Look, I know what I saw and I saw him looking at me like a hungry beast. My brother Walter said the same thing. He said there was definitely sparks flying while we were together."

Tears welled in my eyes as the desperation set in. How in the world would anyone find me? I'd been so stupid to stop in that dark parking lot. Was anyone even looking for me? I'd been so determined to ditch my security that I'd actually played right into this crazy woman's hands. Thank God I'd told my mom that I was going to Mason's but that was where my trail would end. I closed my eyes and wished that this was all a crazy nightmare but when I opened my eyes again, she was still there, staring at me with a frown on her face.

"What's wrong with you?" she said wrinkling her nose.

I shook my head blinking back tears. "Nothing. I just wish I could go home."

"I bet you would," she chuckled. "But that ain't gonna happen."

She walked over to the chair and dropped heavily into it. "Walter will be home soon and then we'll be deciding the best way to deal with you."

My bottom lip began to tremble uncontrollably so I bit it as hard as I could to stop it and also to keep myself from losing it. We sat in silence and I took the opportunity to try to figure out exactly where I was being held. From what I could see, we were in a tiny mobile home that had seen better days. The carpet was threadbare, the walls were dingy and yellow and there was a distinct cat smell emanating from the kitchen area. The couch I was sitting on had a busted spring causing me to lean toward the center. The curtains at the windows were tattered and the door had a broken piece of glass in it which had been repaired by a piece of duct tape. The kitchen sink was piled high with dishes and they had spilled out onto the countertops as well. There were piles of newspapers sitting along every wall. An ancient copy machine was against the wall by the door surrounded by reams of paper and not surprisingly, a box of red marking pens.

The sound of an approaching vehicle made her snap her head toward the window and she smiled. "That'll be Walter...good."

My heart sank at the fact that Walter was here. From what she'd implied, whatever her plans were for me hinged on what he said.

The door opened and I gasped as the thin man from the alleyway walked in carrying a bag of groceries. His greasy hair was slicked over to the side and he was wearing black rimmed glasses on the end of his nose. His eyes met mine just for a moment then he walked to the kitchen and dropped everything onto the counter.

"Walter! I'm so glad you're here!" she said clapping her hands together excitedly.

Walter turned and cast a disapproving look toward her. "Marilyn, you need to calm yourself, woman."

She struggled to get out of the chair. "Walter!" She screeched. "Me, calm myself? Time is of the essence. People are going to be looking for her and we need to figure out what to do with her."

Walter began to unload his bag into the fridge effectively ignoring her. She paced back and forth, watching him with pursed lips. It was obvious she was very anxious to get rid of me.

Finally, when he'd put everything away, he walked over to her. "Sister, you're losing it. You've got her and nobody knows where she is. What's the hurry?"

She bowed out her chest to him and stomped her foot. "I want her gone so I can have what's mine!"

He patted her on the arm almost as if she were a child. "Simmer down. Remember, you've got to be patient. You've waited a long time for this, don't blow it."

She glared long and hard at me and then spun around and went to the door. "I need to check to see if anyone's been tamperin' with the mailbox again. It's probably the FBI. I'll be back in a few minutes."

She crept out the door, looking furtively from side to side then down the steps pulling the door shut behind her.

Within seconds, Walter was next to me and I drew back in fear but in his eyes, I could see sympathy and sadness. "Ms. Charles, I'm so sorry for all this," he said softly. "I know you're scared but I promise you that I'll do all I can to protect you. Marilyn is *special* and once she gets something in her head, it's hard to get it back out." He glanced around to make sure the coast was clear and whispered, "Hopefully she'll get over this and I can get you out of here safely."

Tears sprang to my eyes and I managed to whisper, "Thank you."

Moments later, we heard Marilyn approaching the trailer calling out loudly, "You crazy bastards! I know you're messing with my mailbox. Don't think I don't know!"

Walter dashed back across the room just before Marilyn walked back in carrying stacks of mail. From where I was sitting, I could see they were all marked RETURN TO SENDER. She dropped them on the floor and began pacing back and forth. "How can I get the district attorney to help me get those kids if he won't even open my letters?" She started wringing her hands and mumbling under her breath but I couldn't understand a word she was saying.

Walter handed her a soda with a curly straw. "Here you go, this'll make you feel better." She eyed him suspiciously then took it. "Marilyn, it's just cola, I'm not trying to poison you," he said with a comforting smile.

She took a sip from the straw and smiled. "Ahh, that's good. Thanks, brother." She walked over to her recliner and sat down heavily. "So, do we make it look like a suicide or just an accident?"

My heart instantly leapt to my throat. I glanced over at Walter, who was busily preparing their dinner. "You know, Marilyn? I think we may need a day or two to plan this out…now that we've got her."

She leaned back in the chair and sighed, her eyelids becoming droopy. "You may be right," she said with a yawn.

Walter continued preparing their dinner and watching her closely. When she began to snore loudly, he came to stand beside me. He whispered, "I may be able to at least let someone know you're okay. Who do you want me to contact?"

My mom was the first person who came to mind.

"Please tell my mom, Cara Charles that I'm okay...for now," I said softly. I felt that no matter what Walter said, Marilyn was going to get her way.

Walter nodded and went back to cutting his vegetables. I sat back on the couch and rubbed my eyes with the heel of my hands trying to stop the tears from flowing. We sat in silence for what seemed like an eternity with the only sounds being Marilyn's snores and Walter's clanging of pots and pans.

Suddenly, Marilyn sat straight up in her chair. She looked around wildly until her eyes settled on me. She stood and walked over to the couch and grabbed me tightly by the shoulder. "Let's go for a little walk," she snarled.

Walter's eyes widened and he rushed over to stand beside me. "Sister, you can't go out now. I've got dinner on the table." She glanced over at the pile of steaming food and grunted.

"Oh, all right. But after dinner, me and her are gonna take a walk."

Walter nodded and smiled. "That's fine, sister. You can do that, just come on over to the table and get some dinner in you before you do."

They sat down to eat and despite my desperate situation, my stomach growled uncontrollably at the smell of their dinner since it had been hours since I'd eaten. As they ate, I could hear Walter pleading with her to keep me around a little longer. "You know, she has a lot of money. I bet we could get some of that before you get the kids. Kinda like a ransom, if you know what I mean."

Marilyn sat back in her chair, wiped her face with the back of her arm and burped loudly. "Walter, I like how you think. I'm gonna need money to take care of them young'uns since Rusty didn't leave me nothin' in his will," she said with a rotten smile.

She got up from the table and stretched. "Are you gonna stand guard so I can get some sleep? I'm wore slam out."

Walter jumped to his feet and once again gave me a look that gave me hope that he was on my side. "I'll take care of her, you get some rest. You've had a very busy day!" He took her by the elbow and led her to one of the back rooms. A few moments later, he came out and whispered, "If you promise me you won't run, I'll try to make a call to your mom for you the next time I'm in town." He held up my cell phone just out of my reach. "Oh, and if you're thinking of running, we're way off the main road so you wouldn't get far before Marilyn caught you and I can promise, she wouldn't be as forgiving as I am."

My instinct to flee was foremost in my mind but I suppressed it. The longer I could keep them from harming me increased the odds of someone coming to my rescue. "I promise...and thank you."

He went to the closet and pulled out a pillow and blanket which he handed to me then sat in the chair. I closed my eyes trying to rest so I wouldn't become disoriented from lack of sleep. In my mind, I pictured Gage and Madison and said a silent prayer that I'd see them again and then I thought of my mom and how worried she must be.

I felt something as if someone were watching me and immediately, my eyes popped open and I gasped. Sitting on the edge of the couch was Rusty. He smiled. "Hey, baby."

I glanced around to make sure that Walter didn't hear but he wasn't there. "Rusty? What...how?"

"Baby, I promise you everything's gonna be okay."

I covered my face with my hands. "Rusty, what am I going to do?"

"Have faith," he said. "I'll always be watching over you and the kids. You need to be strong for them. Do you remember when Madison was born? You promised me that you'd move on and live a full and happy life. It pains me to see you unhappy."

"But what am I going to do? How am I going to get out of this?" He didn't answer right away. *"I am going to get out of here, aren't I?"*

"I'm not the only one watching over you. Someone is desperately looking for you so don't give up."

"Mason?" I asked but instead of answering, he started to get up to leave. *"Rusty! Please tell me!"*

He stopped and turned back to me. *"You may feel as if you're broken, but he's the one to heal you. Give him a chance."*

A loud snore from Marilyn startled me and sadly, I realized it had all been a dream.

Chapter 15

Mason

I felt as if I were going to jump out of my skin. It was driving me crazy that we'd had no contact from Ryanne, no leads on the whereabouts of the car.

I'd just wanted to drive around looking for her but I knew that would've just made things worse. I needed to stay with the team and be ready for any news and be able to act on it immediately.

The media got a hold of the story about twelve hours after she disappeared. Cara had confided in a friend and that so-called friend had sold the story to the tabloids as an anonymous source. Within hours, the press had made camp outside the gates of the house reminiscent of when Rusty had died. In the days that followed, they made it nearly impossible for anyone to come or leave the house without being barraged by reporters begging for an update. The news stories started out speculating that she'd run off with Lucas Bryant but when he came forward with his new wife to set the record straight, they scrambled to come up with a new scenario. Cara was devastated that her friend had broken her confidence and sold her story which only deepened the depression she'd sunk into.

It was two in the afternoon and Ryanne had been gone for almost a week and a half. I walked into the kitchen and found Cara in tears as she tried to make a pot of coffee for the team and the volunteers who were milling around the house. Her hands were shaking as she poured me a cup. "Mason, do you think I may have made things worse? I thought she was my friend."

I shook my head no just as her phone rang. She looked at it and a look of relief and joy came over her face. "Oh, my God! It's Ryanne!" My heart leapt. She answered and immediately, her eyes grew big and she gasped. "Who is this?"

I reached toward her to take the phone but she held it tight. "Listen, she's my daughter and I need to know she's okay. Please, can I talk to her?" She listened and her face grew pale. "Why are you doing this?" She sobbed. "Why would you want to hurt her?"

I clenched my hands so tightly that my nails dug into my palms.

"Please, she has children!" she said then a moment later held the phone away from her head. "He hung up."

"What did he say?" I asked with dread.

Her voice was quivering as she said, "He said she's alive and that he wants her to stay that way. He said *he* doesn't want to hurt her but he's not in charge."

"What the hell?" I shouted as I slammed my fist on the counter making Cara flinch as tears filled her eyes.

Afraid of upsetting her further, I quickly pulled myself together. Opening my arms, I hugged her and let her sob against my chest. "We'll find her, I swear it. I've got to trace that phone. Hopefully, they don't realize that they've just given us a clue."

When I got Cara calmed down, I made another quick call to Mike again and gave him an update. He told me that they may be able to trace the signal from Ryanne's phone to the closest tower, which would definitely give me a starting point for my search. Despite my urgency, he informed me that it may take a little while to get the information. After some very frustrated pacing of the kitchen, I decided to go upstairs to her room. Being there, surrounded by her things, gave me a sense of calm. I sat on the edge of the bed and tears began to stream down my cheeks. I closed my eyes and pictured her face, her beautiful face. My heart ached with the notion that I may not ever hold her again. Taking a deep breath, I caught a faint whiff of her perfume and it caused my heart to ache even more. I reached into my pocket and pulled out my phone to check to make sure I didn't miss the call from my friend. Nothing. I buried my face in my hands and began to pray. I prayed that the children would have their mother home safely and that even if she and I weren't meant to be together, that I'd still be able to be a part of her life in some small way.

"Mason?" Upon hearing the tiny voice, my eyes popped open. Gage was standing at the doorway with a look of sadness on his face. "Wh—wha's wrong?"

I held out my hand to him and he rushed over to jump onto my lap. Hugging him close, I said, "Nothing, little man. I had something in my eye."

He looked up at me with a frown but seemed satisfied with my explanation. "Mimi says I need a nap but I don't wanna."

Gathering him up in my arms, I carried him to his bedroom. I let him pick a book and I read to him until he could barely keep his eyes open. When he was safely tucked into his bed, I leaned over and kissed his forehead. "Sleep tight, little man," I whispered.

He looked up at me with blue eyes that mirrored his mothers and smiled. "Love you."

"Love you too," I managed to choke out as I felt the tears coming again so I quickly left the room and almost ran into Cara. "Gage is down for his nap."

She peeked into the room and pulled the door closed. "Thank you. I didn't want him to see me upset. You're really good with him," she said sadly.

I was about to respond when my phone rang. It was Mike. I silently prayed he'd found something we could go on.

I answered. "Mason."

"Hey, man. We got a hit on the tower. It's south of town near where we went hunting last fall. I've got some of the local deputies keeping an eye out for any sign of the car. I'll text you a map of the general area."

"Thanks. I'm on it." A moment later, my phone chimed with the map photo. I enlarged it on my phone and immediately recognized the area. I'd gone there deer hunting with Mike and some of his friends from work. I looked up from my phone and saw Cara's hopeful face. "We may have a lead. I'm going out to see if I can find her."

I called Ryder and gave him the update. He told me that he and Darryl would be joining me in the search and that Joey was going to stick close to the kids in case anyone got any crazy ideas. I kicked my car into gear and headed toward the area we'd gotten our last cell phone ping.

Mike had informed me that the radius I'd need to search was about thirty-five miles and unfortunately, it was mostly rural with some small communities, dirt roads and lots of woods. I rode through the towns hoping to catch a glimpse of our suspect and stopping townsfolk to ask if they knew who he was. Ryder and Darryl were doing the same and despite our excellent coverage, we came up empty. It was beginning to turn dark again and I knew that searching was futile when you just couldn't see where you were going. Reluctantly, I decided to find a motel nearby and resume the search in the morning. The other guys headed back to Charlotte and were going to come back at first light. Checking the hotel app on my phone, I found a decent one and pulled in. I parked in the empty space at the office and after checking in, I made my way to the room and backed my car into the space in front of the door. As I was climbing out, something caught my eye behind the building. I could just barely see the tail end of a car sticking out from behind a dumpster but what got my attention was the color. It was a deep dark burgundy. My heart began to race as I cautiously made my way through the parking lot toward the car. I rounded the dumpster and stopped and took a deep breath. It was Ryanne's car. I made my way toward the driver's side praying that she wasn't dead inside. Instead, I found her purse and the keys laying on the seat but not her. Nervously, I hit the trunk release, again hoping I wouldn't find her there. The trunk was empty.

I called Ryder. "Hey, man, I found the car."

"Where? Any sign of Ryanne?" Ryder asked anxiously.

I sighed. "She's not here. I'm at the Prescott Hotel. I searched the car but only found her purse and keys. I'm going to ask around and see if anyone saw who left this car here."

"Mason, if you find out anything that you think will lead you to her, don't go in alone. Call us and we'll be right there."

"Sure thing," I lied. "I'll let you know before I go anywhere."

"I'll call you in the morning." Ryder hung up and I spun around looking for any clues to where she might have gone.

I went back to the office and rang the bell. The manager came out with a confused expression on his face. "Is there a problem, sir?" he asked nervously.

Just in case he was a part of the whole plot, I played it cool. "No problem, just saw that sweet mustang out in the parking lot and was wondering if you knew who owned it."

He shook his head. "No, I reckon the owner's gonna get it as soon as they get out of jail."

"Jail?" I stared at him.

"Yeah, I saw the cops stop the car over a week ago and then they took the person away. Later that night, I noticed the car had been parked over there but I never saw who moved it. I just assumed that a tow truck would impound it."

I thanked him and as soon as I was outside, I called Mike. "Hey, man, do you have a record of a traffic stop in front of the Prescott Hotel the night Ryanne went missing?"

He put me on hold for a few minutes and then came back. "I don't have any record of a stop by either city, county or highway patrol. Are you sure?"

That didn't make any sense. The hotel manager was sure that it was a police car…or—no it couldn't be. Was it possible Ryanne's captor impersonated a cop? I ran back into the office and rang the bell for the manager.

"Excuse me. Do you have any surveillance cameras out front?" Please say yes, I prayed.

"Uh, yeah. You need to see something?"

I nodded and followed him back into the office. "I need to see the video from the night you saw the cop stop that mustang."

The image wasn't very clear but it was workable. I asked him to start the video from nine that evening since that was the last time Ryanne was seen. I saw a few cars come in and out of the parking lot and then I saw the mustang roll to a stop. It was definitely Ryanne because you could see her in the driver's seat and the convertible top was down. She had her hands covering her face and my heart ached because it was obvious she was crying. A moment later, a dark colored sedan with flashing lights pulled in and parked right behind her. A figure got out of the car holding a flashlight and when the person got to Ryanne, they shined the light directly in her face. She fumbled around for a moment, no doubt looking for her license and registration then she got out. The light was still blinding her making it hard to see the person holding it. She turned to face the car and that's when I saw her struck from behind then crumple to the ground. Another person joined the first and together, they picked her up and carried her to their car. A few minutes later, someone wearing a baseball cap climbed in her car, put the roof up and then parked it where I'd ultimately found it.

I backed the video up and tried to get a better look at the car. It was obviously an older model and from what I could tell, it was four-door since they'd tossed Ryanne into the back seat. I let the video run through again and winced every time I saw Ryanne struck. Whoever had done this to her was most definitely going to pay. I was just about to turn it off when I noticed something I hadn't before. When the two of them carried her to the car, for a brief moment, I saw the silhouette of the first person and it was most definitely a woman.

Something seemed familiar about her short stature and build. Suddenly, it hit me. At the premiere, the thin man had been standing next to a woman maniacally waving an autograph book. Perhaps this woman was the one in the video. *Think, Mason!* I closed my eyes and pictured the man again and then suddenly, another memory came to me…a memory of the news report right after Rusty's accident. I ran to my hotel room, grabbed my laptop and did a search for news stories related to Rusty's accident. After a quick scroll through, I came across the clip featuring the reporter who'd been standing outside the gate.

I clicked on the video and watched praying that I was right.

"Good evening. Tonight the racing world is still reeling from the news that popular driver, Rusty MacNeil was killed in an automobile accident yesterday evening. His widow, Ryanne Charles, has just returned to their home on Lake Norman and was greeted by hundreds of fans and flower arrangements. Excuse me," he said turning to a woman holding a sign that read *Rusty will always be my #1!* "I understand you have been out here ever since the news broke. What did Rusty MacNeil mean to you?"

The woman wiped her eyes with a well-used tissue. "He was so handsome and funny and a hell of a race car driver. He was a nice guy and never wrecked anybody. I don't know if I can watch racing anymore."

The reporter patted her on the shoulder as she broke down in tears. He quickly turned to a man standing nearby, dressed from head to toe in Rusty's team apparel. It was my suspect. "Sir, what does this mean for racing?"

The man cleared his throat, obviously emotional. "I knew Rusty when he was a boy. He'd race anything with wheels. His daddy and I were in business together and we were his first sponsors. I can't believe this happened and my thoughts and prayers go out to Ryanne and Gage."

It was definitely him. The thin man was with a woman who was obsessed with Rusty. He said he'd been his first sponsor which gave me a big break. I did an internet search and found out that Rusty's first sponsor was A & M Salvage. It was owned by Russell MacNeil and Walter Autry. Another image search using the name Walter Autry provided me with a picture of my suspect. I called Ryder but it went to voicemail. I quickly left a message.

"Hey, I got a lead on the thin man. His name is Walter Autry. I'm going to see if I can get an address on him and check it out. I'm praying I'm right and that nothing has happened to Ryanne. I'll keep in touch."

I grabbed my gun and some extra ammo and jumped in the car. A & M Salvage was only twenty miles away.

Chapter 16

Ryanne

The days had dragged on and on. The endless daily threats by Marilyn to take me out and shoot me were countered by Walter with the argument that I was worth a lot of money alive. I felt like my life was literally hanging in the balance between them. Marilyn wanted me to suffer for 'killing' Rusty and ruining her only chance at happiness so she absolutely refused to give me anything to eat but when she went to bed, Walter would sneak me some of the leftovers which I graciously accepted and scoffed down as quickly as possible. The thought that each meal could be my last was prominent in my mind but I also reasoned that if I had to run, I'd need the strength to do it. As the days passed, Marilyn became angrier because she hadn't gotten any closer to getting what she wanted, my kids and a ton of money. She wanted to call and demand both but Walter always persuaded her to wait just a little bit longer. One afternoon, the opportunity came for Walter to leave for supplies but before he did, he secretly tucked my cell phone in his pocket. When he returned an hour or so later, he gave me a nod to let me know he'd done what he promised and then slipped the phone back so Marilyn wouldn't suspect.

Later that night, for the first time since I'd been captured, the silence in the trailer was deafening. Somehow, Marilyn was sleeping in a position where she wasn't snoring which was a blessing. Walter, as usual, was camped out in the recliner but every time I moved, his eyes popped open and he'd shake his head at me. My situation was definitely desperate and the only thing that gave me any peace was the hope that Walter had called and that my mom knew I was okay but that could change at any moment. I prayed that someone was out looking for me but also had to face the reality that finding me may not be the easiest thing to do. I shifted on the couch and once again, Walter's eyes popped open. "You hungry?" he quietly asked.

I really didn't want to admit I was but another round of noises from my stomach answered for me. Walter got up and opened the fridge. He dug around and pulled an apple from the crisper. He cut it up into wedges and walked over to me then held out a slice in front of my face. Reluctantly, I took it with my mouth and as soon as the cold apple hit my tongue, I felt rejuvenated. I ate it quickly and eagerly waited for another slice. I made quick work of the apple and I felt so much better.

"Thank you. I know you didn't have to do that," I said gratefully.

He shrugged. "I'm not an animal. Now, my sister? Different story."

"May I ask you a question?"

He nodded with another shrug. "Sure."

"Do you think I'm going to get out of here alive?"

He didn't answer right away and I felt prickles up and down my spine. Finally, he walked away to the kitchen to put the plate away. "I don't really know. Marilyn's unpredictable."

Tears welled in my eyes. "You would let her take me from my children?"

He shuffled over to his chair and sat down. "Nobody lets Marilyn do anything. She just does it. That's why I'm trying to stick close to you. I'm afraid if I leave for too long, she'll make good on her promise to take you for a walk in the woods and..."

I closed my eyes and tried to keep the images of my kids in my mind. They were the only thing keeping me from losing it completely.

Walter dropped back in his chair and reclined it then flipped on the television. "Well, now that I'm wide awake, I might as well see the latest news on your disappearance."

I listened breathlessly as the reporter recounted the two week timeline since I'd been missing and the theories of why I'd gone. Two weeks? Had it been that long? The news anchors were discussing the story that implied that I'd run off with Lucas and then they said that they had an exclusive statement from Lucas himself. He emphatically denied we were together and then introduced the reporter to his new wife Trina. The weather and sports followed then the newscast ended and an infomercial began and within moments, I'd dozed off.

The distant sound of a dog barking woke me and I saw that it had woken Walter as well. He jumped from his chair and pulled back the curtains but obviously couldn't see anything because of the darkness. He motioned for me to stay put and reaching behind the chair, pulled out a shotgun. He checked the barrel for ammo then snapped it shut and slowly opened the door. He crept out pulling the door closed behind him. A moment later, Marilyn came stumbling into the room.

"What the hell is going on? Where's Walter?" she demanded.

"I don't know. He heard a dog barking and went to check on it," I answered truthfully.

She grabbed me roughly by the arm and pulled me to my feet. "Let's go. The only time that dog barks is when someone is snooping around the junkyard." She grabbed the flashlight and that's when I saw the small pistol tucked into the waistband of her jeans. She pushed me to the door and opened it cautiously. "Walter? You out there?" She hissed.

There was only silence. She pushed me roughly down the concrete block steps causing me to stumble and fall into the dirt. Yanking me up by the elbow, she propelled me toward the woods as she glanced nervously around for any signs of Walter. I tried to keep my footing but because it was so dark, I kept losing my balance. Marilyn was trying to hold the flashlight to see her way and keep a tight grip on my forearm as we went deeper and deeper into the woods. The sky brightened slightly as the clouds cleared revealing the light from the moon which made it a bit easier to walk without tripping. Suddenly, she stopped and yanked me to a halt and listened. She hissed at me to sit on the trunk of a fallen tree. The barking had ceased and the only sound was from the crickets and the occasional hoot from an owl. My heart was thundering in my ears as the desperation and fear gripped me. Regret washed over me as I realized that this could be my last moment on earth. My babies were foremost in my mind and then I thought of Mason. Sitting here on this log in the middle of the woods with a lunatic, I realized how much I loved him. I'd loved him all along, first as a friend and then as a lover but I'd let my fear of moving on keep me back and I'd let him go…right back into the arms of his ex.

Marilyn was becoming more and more agitated. Every little sound was making her jump. Suddenly we heard a loud crash close by. "What was that?" she whispered as she pulled the gun from her waistband. She swung the flashlight beam through the woods, her eyes searching for any movement. "Walter?" Her hands and voice were trembling as she spun around in a circle. Just to our left, the crack of a stick breaking as someone approached made her drop the flashlight into the thick brush, partially extinguishing its light. "Walter, is that you?"

"Yup," he answered from the darkness. Relief flooded over me because I knew that he would try to keep Marilyn from hurting me. My eyes had adjusted a little and I could just make out Marilyn standing beside me still holding the gun. She lowered it and began to slide it back into her pants when all of a sudden, Walter tackled her to the ground knocking the breath out of her. At first, I was so shocked at what I was seeing that I didn't even try to run but then my instincts kicked in and I leapt from the log and took off running. I'd gone a few feet and I realized that I didn't have a clue which way to go so I headed deeper into the woods hoping to lose them both.

I crashed through the trees and underbrush until my side hurt and I finally had to stop and catch my breath. Looking up at the sky, I saw a brief break in the clouds which gave me enough light to search for a place to hide. About five feet to my right was another broken tree which had a small gap under it. As quietly as I could, I ducked down and crawled under using my elbows to propel myself since my hands were still bound. I tucked my feet under me and tried to quiet my heavy breathing. A few minutes later, I heard footsteps approaching and I held my breath to conceal myself. They grew closer and closer until I heard them stop right beside me.

"Ryanne!"

My breath came out in a whoosh and I cried out, "Mason!"

I peered out and saw Mason kneeling at the entrance to my hideout. He held out his hand to me and I grabbed on tightly then he gently eased me toward him. Once I was able to stand, he wrapped his arms around me and pulled me close. He murmured against my hair, "Oh, my God, I've got you. It's okay, baby. I've got you."

My legs felt like jelly and I collapsed against him and began to sob. "Mason, is it really you? Is this a dream?"

He squeezed me tighter. "I'm here. It's really me." He pulled out a knife and cut my bindings then scooped me up into his arms and carried me through the woods to the yard outside the trailer. A few minutes later, an SUV came roaring down the dirt road then skidded to a stop. Ryder and Darryl jumped from the truck and came running toward us.

"Where are they?" Ryder asked brandishing his gun.

Mason pointed to the shed behind the trailer. "The guy is in there and his accomplice is handcuffed to a tree in the woods about two hundred yards in."

Darryl nodded and headed toward the woods while Ryder went to the shed. He opened the door and found Walter tied up and gagged inside. He pulled him out and walked him to the SUV. Moments later, several police cars with sirens screaming pulled up next to Ryder's truck. The officers took custody of Walter and a few minutes later, Darryl came from the woods pushing Marilyn out in front of him. "Here's the other one," he said handing her over to the police officer.

Marilyn snatched her arm free and came rushing toward me. "YOU BITCH! I'LL GET YOU!" she screamed.

Mason quickly pushed me behind him blocking me from her swinging fists. The officers subdued her and pulled her toward the police car. She resisted when they tried to push her into the car but they were finally able to get her inside and they slammed the door. As they drove away, she began to scream and bang her head against the window.

Ryder and Darryl walked to us. "Mason, we're going to head to the station and do some reports. They're going to need Ryanne at the station for a statement but we'll stall them so you can have some time together."

As I watched them leave, relief that the ordeal was over washed over me. Mason pulled me into his arms and held me tightly and slowly, my trembling subsided. "Mason, I was so stupid –" He put his finger to my lips and shook his head.

"No, you're not stupid. Those two had a very elaborate plan. You were followed and if you hadn't stopped at that motel parking lot, they would have gotten you somewhere else."

"How did you find me?"

He stroked my cheek with his fingertips. "It wasn't easy but after Walter called your mom, it gave us an area to search. I lucked out by finding your car at the motel The manager just happened to see you get stopped which gave me a timeline. We ran the security video and saw the entire thing go down and suddenly, things began to click into place. The video showed a woman and a thin man and that's when I remembered a news story that ran right after we came back from Wilmington. Your captors were interviewed standing outside the gates of the house and it turns out that Walter Autry was a partner in a salvage yard with Rusty's dad and they sponsored his first race car. I tracked down the address to the business and met a pretty ferocious Doberman guarding the fence. I managed to get him distracted long enough to get through and that was when I saw Walter coming to see what the dog was barking at."

"I hope you didn't hurt him, he never wanted to harm me," I said softly.

He kissed my forehead. "No, I didn't hurt him. Actually, as soon as he saw me, he dropped the gun and held out his hands for the cuffs. He told me that you were in the trailer and that if I wore his hat as a disguise, his sister Marilyn would be caught off guard. Unfortunately, when I got there, you were gone. Luckily, I was only moments behind you and could follow without being detected. When you stopped, Marilyn dropping the flashlight gave me the perfect opportunity to make my move."

"I really thought you were Walter."

"That's what I wanted Marilyn to believe too. When I tackled her and cuffed her to the tree, I turned around and you were gone. I just started running hoping that I was going the same way that you'd gone and began calling out your name."

"That was the sweetest sound I've ever heard," I admitted with a smile.

He smiled and held my bruised wrist to his lips. "The sweetest sound for me was you saying my name."

"Mason, I know this isn't probably the best time to say this but I'm sorry." He frowned but I continued, "I know it's too late for us but I hope that you and your wife will have a long and happy life together."

He didn't say anything, he just stood staring at me, his brows drawn together. I looked away but he turned my face back toward him with his fingertips. "Listen, I don't know what you heard at my apartment," he said shaking his head. "Nothing, I repeat nothing is going on with Kristin and me. She showed up at my place fully intending to get me back but I made it clear that my heart belongs to someone who deserves it...you."

I looked into his beautiful blue eyes and saw nothing but love in them. "Mason, can you ever forgive me?"

"Forgive you? You did nothing wrong. You loved someone with all of your heart and fate stepped in and took him from you way too soon. You were broken and I hoped that in time, you'd be able to live again and especially love again. I pushed you too hard and I know that's why you slept with me."

My face flushed. "That's not it at all. Mason, you were my friend and like an idiot, I took you for granted and then ruined everything by forcing you to sleep with me."

He smiled. "Is that what you think? You think you forced me? Baby, I was more than willing. The only thing I wanted was for you not to feel any regret or guilt but you did and it put up a wall between us. I knew you weren't ready for a relationship so I stepped out of the picture to give you time to figure out what you wanted."

I reached up to stroke his cheek with my thumb. "Sometimes, you have to open your eyes to see the only thing you need is right in front of you."

"Ryanne, are you saying –?"

"Yes, Mason, I'm saying that I love you."

His eyes searched my face then he slid his fingers into my hair and pulled my lips to his. His broad hand spanned the small of my back and he pulled me tightly against him. Our lips brushed softly at first then became more demanding, and a soft moan escaped from my mouth. I clutched at his shoulders and felt myself being lifted up and I instinctively wrapped my legs around his waist. He carried me that way to the car and gently sat me on the hood. He nuzzled against my neck then whispered, "As much as I'd love to stay with you like this forever, we've got to go to the police station so we can get that out of the way."

He opened my car door and helped me get in. My body tingled with excitement watching him walk around the car to climb in beside me. When we arrived at the station, I was taken to an interview room and had to recount everything that had happened from the time I left my house. Despite the fact that Walter had in fact been a part of my abduction, I felt some compassion toward him for trying to help me while still keeping his sister happy. Marilyn was obviously delusional and I knew that she would have hurt me if she'd gotten the opportunity. I told the police everything and asked them to give Walter some leniency with regard to the charges against him.

A few hours later, when I was free to leave, I found Mason waiting patiently. He gathered me into his arms and held me tightly. "It's really late. I called your mom and told her you were safe. Are you ready to go home?"

"Mason, can we go to your place so I can clean up? I don't want my mom or my kids to see me like this."

"Of course." He took me by the arm and led me to the car. We drove the few blocks to his apartment in silence. When we arrived, he ran around to my door, opened it and reached in to carry me from the car.

"Mason, I *can* walk!" I protested weakly. I actually enjoyed his massive arms carrying me so easily. When he arrived at his apartment door, he shifted me slightly so he could unlock the door and then carried me into his apartment. The first thing that struck me was how truly manly this place was. It was sparsely furnished but every piece of furniture had a purpose. No decorative knick-knacks for Mason, just the basic apartment furnishings. He kicked the door closed with his foot and quickly locked it behind us. He strode to the bedroom and gently set me on my feet.

I stifled a yawn and immediately flushed with embarrassment. Mason kissed me softly and then walked over to his wardrobe. He pulled out an oversized t-shirt and some boxers and handed them to me. "Baby, you are going to put these on and then you're going to get some much needed sleep. I'll take you home in the morning."

I started to protest but he shook his head, turned me to the bathroom and patted me gently on my rear. After closing the door, I quickly slipped out of my grimy clothes and climbed into the hot shower. It felt fantastic to be clean and when I stepped out of the shower and I looked in the mirror, my reflection showed my fatigue but there was something else. My eyes no longer were dull and lifeless but instead were bright. I slipped on Mason's shirt and boxers as I finished up and when I opened the door, the lights were dimmed and Mason was laying on the bed and holding the covers open for me. The sheets were cool against my heated skin causing me to shiver. He protectively tucked me against him and he kissed the back of my shoulder and then pulled my hair away from my neck so he could place soft kisses there as well. I felt so safe and within moments, I was fast asleep.

Chapter 17

Mason

The light of morning began to stream through the openings in the blinds and I could see Ryanne was still fast asleep. She was making a tiny snoring noise that I found absolutely adorable and I lay watching her for about an hour before she began to stir. She'd been wrapped in my arms all night and never moved. My arm had gone to sleep at some point but I didn't care one bit. She was here and that was all that mattered. Her eyelashes fluttered and she opened her eyes then began to stretch. She turned her head to face me and asked with a smile, "Are you real?" With a grin, I nodded and kissed her cheek. She rolled over and we were nose to nose with her hands tucked against my bare chest. "I'm glad you're here."

Tucking a strand of hair behind her ear, I whispered, "There's nowhere I'd rather be."

She kissed me softly. "Thank you for saving me."

"If I'd lost you –" My voice cracked with emotion.

"Shh, I'm okay…despite my complete lack of sense. I shouldn't have gone running around all by myself. Especially knowing some nut job was out there waiting for me."

"It's all over now, thank God. And as much as I'd love to lay here with you all day, I need to get you home." We crawled from the bed and I dug around in my drawers for something clean she could wear home. She grabbed a couple of things and dashed to the bathroom to change and I made some coffee.

A few minutes later, she came out of the bathroom braiding her hair. "Mm, that coffee smells so good." Pouring a cup for each of us, I handed her a steaming mug and then took a drink from my own. She took a sip and moaned. "This is so good. You always did know how to make a mean cup of coffee.

"Thank you, ma'am. I do my best," I said with a bow.

She sat her cup down on the counter and her expression grew serious. "Mason, I need to talk to you before we go to the house."

Crossing my arms, I leaned back against the counter. "Okay."

"This is really awkward," she murmured looking down at her cup.

"Ryanne, say what's on your mind."

"Well, I want you to come home with me…to be *with* me. But at the same time, I want you to be my protector, my security. You're the only person I truly trust to take care of the kids and me. How can I have it both ways?"

I smiled and held out my hand to her. "Come here." She walked over to stand in front of me still keeping her eyes downcast. Sliding my hand around the nape of her neck, I pulled her to me until our foreheads met. "Ryanne, you and the kids mean more to me than anything. I'm willing to do whatever it takes to be with you and make you happy." Her eyes met mine and I melted inside. She was just so damn beautiful. "I know what you're thinking…I need a job and if I'm taking care of you, then I'm really working for you." She nodded sadly. "What you don't know is that I really don't have to work."

She frowned. "What do you mean?"

Reaching around her waist with my other hand, I pulled her tightly against me. "You really don't know a lot about me, only that I was a cop and I was married. I really haven't shared much and it's time you find out. My dad was Stanford Leffler. I know that name probably doesn't mean anything to you but–"

She gasped. "THE Stanford Leffler?"

I chuckled. "Yeah, that's what everyone called him. When I was a kid, I thought his first name was 'THE'. Obviously, you recognized his name."

"Well, everyone in the motion picture business would know that name. Every movie he produced ended up becoming a blockbuster."

I shrugged. "I was hoping you'd never put the connection together with me because truthfully, I tried to disconnect myself from him after I was an adult. He was very controlling and wanted me to follow in his footsteps as CEO of his production company. As soon as I was old enough to move out, I left and joined the police academy. He was so angry that he wouldn't speak to me and also forced my mother to do the same. What he didn't know was that she called me behind his back to make sure that I was okay. She didn't like me being a cop because it was so dangerous but I loved it. When I got shot, they rushed me to the hospital and the first person there, to my surprise, was my dad."

"What did he say?"

"He told me he was proud of the man I'd become and he apologized for being so stubborn."

"So, what happened then?"

I closed my eyes and took a deep breath. "He was diagnosed with cancer six months after we reconciled. Six months after that, he was gone."

"Oh God, I'm so sorry. And your mom?"

"About a year after Dad died, she had a stroke and ended up in a nursing facility for about a three months before she passed away."

"Mason, I'm so sorry. It had to have been terrible to lose both of your parents."

"It was but it also taught me a valuable lesson. Make each day count and tell the important people in your life how you feel about them." I kissed her lightly on the lips.

"You're so right. Losing Rusty was the hardest thing I've ever had to face in my life but it's also made me realize that life is so fleeting and unpredictable. I don't want to miss out on a beautiful future by holding on to the past." She wiped a tear from her eye and then held me tight.

"So, the point of telling you this was to let you know that I'm pretty financially secure. I work because I want to and if you want me to be there for you day…and night," I said with a grin. "Then I'll do it."

She kissed me softly. "I do."

I took her hand in mine and brought it to my lips. "Then let's go home."

As we drove onto her street, the crowds that were milling around the gate began to cheer. Cameras were flashing and people were crowding around the car as I stopped to enter the gate code.

"We love you!"

"Thank God you're safe!"

Ryanne waved to the crowds and was met with even more cheers.

We drove to the house and when we pulled up to the house, the front door flew open and Gage came running out followed closely by Cara who was carrying Madison. "Mama!" Gage squealed.

Ryanne threw open the door and ran toward him. "Baby!" She scooped him into her arms and peppered his face with kisses.

"Mama, I missed you!" Gage was gripping her tightly around the neck and as I drew closer, I saw tears streaming down her cheeks. Cara was crying as well so I took Madison from her so she could wrap her arms around Ryanne as well.

When they broke their hug, Ryanne turned to us. "Hey, little one," she said as she took her from my arms. Madison gave her a sloppy kiss as she wrapped her little arms around her neck.

"We're so glad you're home," Cara said wiping her eyes. She looked over at me and mouthed, *Thank you!*

"Mom, can you take Madison for a moment? I need to help Mason bring his bags in."

Her eyes grew wide and I saw the hint of a smile. "Why certainly! I'm glad to hear he's coming back."

Ryanne linked her hand with mine. "Well, he's not coming back to work."

Her mouth fell open. "Do you mean what I think you mean?"

When we both nodded she clapped her hands with delight. "Oh, I'm so happy for you both." She quickly took the kids into the house leaving us alone.

"I guess we're really doing this," I said pulling her close.

She lay her head on my chest as she wrapped her arms around my waist. "I'm scared but I'm ready. Let's get you moved back in."

I grabbed the bags from the trunk and once inside the house, despite Ryanne's protests, I put them into my room. When I saw her disappointment, I quickly explained. "It's not that I don't want to share your room…I do. It's just that I want the kids to get used to me being here again before we move to the next level."

"So, Mr. Leffler, are you asking me to be your girlfriend?" she asked with a coy smile.

I nodded. "As a matter of fact, I am. I'd like to take you and the kids out to dinner tonight, if that's okay with you."

She laughed. "Are you sure you want to take us on? We can be quite a handful."

"I've never been so sure about anything," I said truthfully.

She cocked her head to one side. "Well, then you've got yourself a date."

She sauntered off leaving me wanting nothing more than to pull her in my arms and kiss her until she was breathless but this was the time to exercise patience.

Ryder came to the house and we went over what happened with the Autry's. He told me that at their arraignment, the judge had been told about Ryanne's request when charging Walter but by law, he had to be charged with being an accessory to a kidnapping. Marilyn had been charged with kidnapping, attempted murder and communicating threats. Both she and Walter had been denied any kind of bond which was a relief to me. When I told Ryder that I was going to be staying in a non-professional capacity at the house, he slapped me on the back and grinned. "I kinda expected this."

"You did?" I asked with surprise.

"Mason, I do background checks on everyone who works for me. Did you think the fact you were Stanford Leffler's son was a secret? You can find out anything if you know where to search."

"So, you're not mad at me?"

He laughed. "Mad at you for being happy? Hell no! You both are deserving of a happy future."

I looked over at Ryanne, who was playing with the kids and smiled. "I love her, man. When I thought I might lose her…I almost lost my mind."

Ryder nodded somberly. "I know exactly how you feel. Marco almost stole the one person who completes me but thank God that didn't happen."

Ryanne looked over at us and gave me a smile and my heart melted. Ryder and I were lucky men to have the love of such amazing women.

Later that night, after everyone had gone to bed, Ryanne and I sat in the den on the couch watching the news. She lay back against me then pulled my arms around her. "I feel so safe," she said looking up at me.

I gave her a squeeze and kissed her forehead. "I'm never letting you go."

We heard a thumping noise and both turned to look up the stairs. Gage was dragging his tattered teddy bear down the stairs behind him as he rubbed his eyes. "Mama? I can't sleep," he cried.

I tried to get up before he saw us wrapped around each other but he was too fast, but instead of being upset, he walked over and climbed up on the couch and cuddled us both. "Mason? I think there's a monster under my bed," he said very seriously.

I ruffled his hair. "Well, let's go see." I carried him upstairs to his room with Ryanne following close behind. When we got to the door, Gage hid his head against my shoulder.

"Do you see him?" he whispered.

"Let me go in and check. Hang out with your mom for a minute." I handed him to Ryanne and went into the darkened room. A moment later I came back out. "I think I'm going to need some monster spray. I'll be right back."

Gage peeked at me and nodded against his mom's neck. "Hurry," he whispered.

I ran downstairs to the kitchen and found an empty spray bottle. I filled it with water then searched the cabinets and came across some eucalyptus oil. I added a couple of drops, shook it up and then with a marker, wrote MONSTER SPRAY on the outside. Dashing back upstairs, I found them in the same spot and when Gage saw what I had in my hand, he lifted his head and watched me enter the room again.

I turned on the light and knelt in front of his bed. As loudly as I could without waking Madison, who was sleeping peacefully in the next room, I said, "Monster be gone!" A couple of quick sprays under the bed then I was off to the closet. Following the same routine there, I then went over to his toy box. I lifted the lid and repeated the process. When I was finished, I turned to find Gage was now standing beside his mom holding her hand. "It's all clear, buddy." I held out my hand to him and he slowly came to me. I handed him the bottle and told him that he could use it every night to make sure they didn't come back.

He looked up at me and smiled. "Thanks. I love you!"

I scooped him up into my arms and hugged him tightly. "I love you too." Gently placing him into his bed, I pulled the covers up around him, tucked his teddy next to him and gave him a kiss on the forehead. Ryanne kissed him goodnight and by the time we'd reached the door, he was fast asleep.

Ryanne pulled me down the hallway to my room. She closed the door quietly and turned to me with tears in her eyes. "That was amazing. Thank you so much for making him feel safe." She wrapped her arms around my waist and held me tightly.

I tilted her chin up to face me. "I would do anything for you."

Her mouth curled into a grin. "I'll hold you to that."

Chapter 18

Ryanne

Shutting my door behind me, I leaned against it and sighed. Watching Mason and Gage together had been magical but for a moment, Rusty had popped into my mind and my heart had literally ached.

Fighting back tears, I wandered into the closet and stared at the boxes that were still piled up from the night I'd begun to pack his things away. Suddenly, I was reminded of the paper I'd found in his tux. I quickly found it and read it over and over closing my eyes and trying to picture Rusty saying the words to me but instead I could only see Mason. Our wedding picture was on the nightstand and when I picked it up, I saw a beautiful couple who'd loved each other completely and made a wonderful family. I wanted the feeling again of being someone's whole world and I knew Mason was willing to give me that.

The next morning, I went downstairs and could hear Mason and my mom talking in the kitchen.

My mom was saying, "I don't think she needs to see this."

Mason replied, "It's going to be impossible to keep it from her."

When I walked into the kitchen, they both turned and I saw my mom turn off her iPad. "What are you keeping from me?" I asked.

She shrugged. "Nothing. It's really nothing." I could see she was hiding something.

"Mason, what's going on?"

He sighed and turned on the iPad. The website they'd been looking at popped back onto the screen. It showed a grainy photo of what appeared to be Mason and me embracing in my driveway. It accompanied a story with the headline, *Finding Love Again.* I quickly skimmed the story which had been totally fabricated. When I saw the name of the person who wrote it, I flipped. It was Zane

Baxter, the jerk who'd upset me during the interview in California.

I read on.

They say I have a nose for news, well this time I hit the nail on the head! While Ryanne Charles was in California for the premiere of her latest movie, I had the opportunity to interview her in her suite at her hotel. Immediately, I noticed the hunky bodyguard watching her every move and I said to myself, "Zane, there's a story there!" Well, it turns out I was right! Hunky bodyguard (whose name is Mason Leffler, sole heir to the Leffler fortune) has apparently been guarding Ms. Charles day and more importantly night. We here at Celebrity Stalker want to share everything with you so enjoy the unedited video of my interview.

A video was inserted into the story and with dread, I clicked on it.

"So, Ryanne Charles, first let me offer my sincere condolences on the loss of your husband, Rusty. I know you've been dealing with some serious and painful issues

and I want you to know that we at Celebrity Stalker all send our best."

"Thank you, Zane. It has been hard."

"We understand you're in Los Angeles for the premiere of your new movie "War of Love" which is set during the Civil War. Do you feel a stronger connection to your character, Lucy Marshall, now that you're a widow like she is in the movie?"

"Ex...excuse me?"

"We understand that your character becomes a widow and we wondered if you felt a closer connection to her now."

"Zane, I understood the question the first time and I really don't feel it's appropriate."

"My apologies, we'll move on. Okay, it's been a few months since you...um...how can I phrase this...became single? Have you thought of finding love again?"

"Are you freaking serious? I didn't 'become single', my husband died. I think this whole line of

questioning is very disrespectful and frankly, Zane, I'm
disappointed in you."

I watched myself rip the microphone from my collar
and run from the room. A moment later, Mason raced into
the room and roared, "You son of a bitch. You think you
can come in here and upset her like that?"

Zane shrank back behind one of the cameramen but
Mason easily reached around and grabbed him by the shirt.
The crew, knowing it was in their best interest, backed
away leaving Zane at Mason's mercy but they never
stopped filming.

Mason lifted Zane from the floor and effortlessly
slammed him against the wall. A picture that was hanging
on the wall shattered and glass fell to the floor. Mason
turned to the person who was filming and seconds later,
the video ended.

The next portion of the video was filmed in the
lobby. Zane was straightening his shirt and picking glass
from his hair. "I should press charges against that maniac!
He's lucky I don't!" The crew was snickering behind his
back and moments later, he screeched, "Are you still

filming? Turn that damn thing off!" After the video ended, I looked up and found my mom and Mason watching me carefully.

I sighed. "Well, that went well."

Mason moved to stand behind me then placed his hands on my shoulders. "So, what's next?"

I knew just what to do. I picked up my phone, called my agent and when he answered, I said, "I know you've seen the crap they're spreading about me, get me on the circuit. I'm going to take care of this myself."

After I hung up, I explained. "The circuit is all the top talk shows. I'm not going to let a tabloid throw out whatever trash they want about me." I turned to Mason. "I understand if you want to keep out of this but I'm prepared to tell everyone that I've found someone who makes me happy and that it's okay."

My mom smiled. "I think that's a wonderful idea. There'll be some who think you've moved on too soon and others who will support you. This is when you find out who your friends are."

"I do need to call Rusty's parents and tell them myself. It's only right."

"I agree," she said taking her iPad. "I'm going to go read for a little while. And NOT Celebrity Stalker." Chuckling, she left us alone.

I felt a knot in my stomach as I dialed their number but as soon as his mom answered, she said, "Ryanne! It's so good to hear from you. Your mother kept us updated during your entire ordeal. We're so grateful to Mason for saving you."

"I am too," I said glancing up to meet Mason's eyes.

"Russell and I were shocked that Walter was involved. He always seemed like a nice man. We knew he had a sister with mental problems but had no idea how dangerous she really was. We hope they didn't hurt you."

"No, thank goodness. Walter was the only reason I wasn't hurt though. Marilyn wanted to kill me every day but luckily he talked her out of it."

"Oh, my God. That's so horrible. I can't imagine how scared you were."

"I was scared but I just kept focusing on the people I love and it helped me get through."

"Speaking of people you love–"

I cut her off. "Um, that's why I called you. I–"

She cut me off in return. "Honey, we saw the story on Celebrity Stalker and honestly, we're so happy for you. We know Rusty would want you to be happy and we feel the same way."

Tears welled in my eyes. "I should've told you before it hit the news but apparently they've been camping outside of my gate."

"That's one of the downsides of living in a fishbowl but just remember, the life you live behind closed doors is the one that counts."

"I love you both so much. I hope you'll come see us soon. The kids would love it."

"We'll do that. We love you like a daughter and always will. Be sure to give Gage and Madison kisses from us. And please tell Mason how grateful we are."

"I will. Talk to you again, soon. Goodbye."

Mason hugged me to him. "They're good people," he said, his voice tight with emotion. "I know that was hard for you to do."

I rested my cheek against his hand. "It was hard but somehow, in my heart, I knew they'd understand. The rest of the world? Who knows?"

Mason and I spent the rest of the day with the kids. We packed a picnic and ate our lunch down on the dock watching the boats go by. Mason looked in the boathouse and found a fishing pole so he took Gage to dig up some worms. They baited their hook and sat together patiently waiting for a bite. What seemed like an eternity later, the pole jumped and Mason quickly jerked it to set the hook. With Gage sitting between his legs, he helped him reel in a pretty good-sized fish. Gage was thrilled and when he held it up to Madison and me, she clapped and babbled something that sounded like 'goo'.

We had an amazing day and for the entire time, I'd left the world behind but when we came into the house, I saw my abandoned phone filled with messages. They were texts from friends asking if the story was true. There was no way I could answer them all but one caught my eye. It was from Lucas. It read, *Rusty would want you to live and love again. I'm here for you always.*

It was so comforting knowing that he understood. He and Rusty had been like brothers and I used to tease them that they shared the same brain. In a way, having Lucas approve was confirmation that I was doing the right thing.

I deleted some more messages and then saw my agent's name pop up. I played the voicemail that informed me I was booked on the morning flight to New York and I was scheduled to appear on several shows. When Mason came in the door with Gage after they'd cleaned the fish, I told him the plan.

"Of course, I'm going with you. I need to get my ticket." he said holding Gage up to the sink to wash his hands. I didn't reply. I just walked over and set some papers on the counter. "What's that?"

I slipped my arm around his waist. "Two tickets to New York."

My mom volunteered to stay a little longer to help Mrs. Jamison with the kids which prompted my dad to take some time off of work to come visit as well. I promised him that after the New York trip he could have Mom back but also made it clear how invaluable she'd been for me through everything that had happened.

The next morning, Mason and I boarded a plane bound for New York City. We were greeted at the airport by Sabrina Toomey, an assistant on the 'Shay' show which was my first stop on the circuit. I was scheduled to appear there for a taping, do a couple of morning shows, then rush over to 'The Coffee Clatch' for an interview with Rowan Harrison. Sabrina got us settled into the Four Seasons and rather than risk a mob at the hotel, we ate a quiet dinner in our room. Later, we sat on the terrace with a glass of wine as we listened to the sounds of the city down below.

"Mm, there's something so exciting about New York," I sighed.

Mason took my hand and held it to his lips. "I can't believe we're here…together."

I turned to him. "Are you ready for tomorrow? Things are going to change and I don't know if they'll be for the better."

He smiled. "As long as I have you, I can face anything."

"You know they'll be digging for anything they can find about you. They'll probably track down Kristin too."

He shrugged. "Let them. She has her own skeletons to deal with."

I lay my head back against the chair. "I've no doubt I'm going to lose friends. People are bound to be uncomfortable with a widow moving on."

"Then they weren't true friends. There are thousands of women and men who lose a partner every day. Are they supposed to live alone for the rest of their lives? Are you damaged goods? I don't think so."

"I guess the stigma is that you've forgotten the person who's no longer here. What they don't realize is that I have two beautiful living and breathing memories of my husband. Gage and Madison remind me every day of their dad. I can keep his memory alive for them through pictures and videos but I can't bring him back."

"Ryanne, people don't know unless they've walked in your shoes. I'm pretty confident that you'll find more support than you expect."

The wine was making me sleepy and I stifled a yawn. Mason stood and pulled me to my feet. "Time for bed." He led me to the bedroom and at the door, he stopped and pulled me to him. "I'm sleeping on the couch," he murmured against my forehead. "You get some sleep and I'll see you in the morning."

"But–"

"Baby, I want to sleep with you more than you'll ever know but tonight, you need your rest and I also need to give you time to think about how much of your life you're willing to share with the public."

He was right. I needed to think about what point I wanted to make by going on all of these shows. Did I want to invite the public into my life, into my bedroom or did I want to keep our relationship under wraps? It was my call, he'd made that clear.

I kissed him goodnight and reluctantly went to bed alone.

The next morning, Mason knocked on the door then brought in a tray full of wonderful breakfast items. "I took the liberty of ordering some of everything that you love."

I took a plate from the tray and filled it with eggs and bacon and took a bright red apple to finish it off. Mason poured me some coffee and sat on the edge of the bed. "Did you sleep okay?"

"Sort of. I kept thinking about you on the couch and was so tempted to go out and join you but I knew you were right. I needed time to get my thoughts together. Putting this trip together was really impulsive and I didn't really think it through until last night."

"Well, today's the day. I'm sure you'll do fine." He took our empty dishes out as I took a quick shower. I didn't have to put on makeup because the show's makeup people were going to take care of all that when I arrived.

Mason knocked and let me know that the car was downstairs so I grabbed my purse and we headed down to the street. As soon as we walked out the door, a passerby recognized me despite the large sunglasses I'd thrown on as we left the lobby.

"Ms. Charles! Is that really you? Can I get a picture with you?" A young woman asked with a small wave.

"Sure," I said moving to stand next to her. She held up her phone and I huddled close as she snapped a picture.

"Thank you so much! I'm a big fan!" She gushed. "Are you doing a project here in New York?"

"No, just some talk shows. I'd love to stay and chat but we need to get going." We left her standing on the street waving enthusiastically as we drove away.

We pulled behind the building where the 'Shay' show was taped and I was whisked in through the crowd that was milling around the door waiting to catch a glimpse of the guests. I heard the squeals as we passed through the door and I had to smile.

I spent about thirty minutes in hair and makeup and then Mason and I were escorted to the green room. There were several large monitors in the room that would show the taping. Shay had two other guests besides me and as she announced their names, the audience went wild but when she announced that I was a guest, there were some cheers and also I detected a few gasps as well. Since the Celebrity Stalker had broken the story, several other tabloids had put their spin on my life situation. People were curious and as I sat there watching their reaction, I realized it was part of my 'job' to let them get to know me. I didn't want them to come to camp out at my house but I wanted them to realize that I was a human being with feelings.

Mason paced the floor and kept glancing at me to make sure I was okay. I was perfectly calm and fully prepared to go out there and say what I'd come to say.

The door to the green room opened and Sabrina popped her head in. "Ms. Charles? We have about five minutes before you go on. I'm here to escort you to the set."

Mason stood and smiled. "Good luck," he said giving me a kiss on the cheek mindful of Sabrina's presence.

I followed her to the set and heard Shay begin my introduction.

"My next guest is one of my absolute favorite actresses. She's been in some of the most successful movies in Hollywood history and just recently, she lived through some of the most traumatic events you could ever imagine. Please welcome, Ryanne Charles!"

The audience began to applaud wildly as I walked out to join Shay on the stage. We hugged and she whispered in my ear, "I'm so happy you're safe."

We sat in the oversized chairs that served as her set and she placed her hand on my arm. "Ryanne, let me first start by saying that you look radiant." She turned to the audience. "Doesn't she?"

The applause rang out again and there were some shouts of 'We love you!' as I waved and smiled.

"Okay, let's get down to it. You told my producers that no subject was taboo so I'm going to jump in. The kidnapping…tell us what happened."

I recounted the events without divulging too much that could possibly hinder the case against Marilyn. "Marilyn Autry is not well. She created fantasies revolving around my late husband and essentially blamed me for his death. I became a target and unfortunately, I walked right into their trap."

"Did they intend to harm you?" she asked with concern.

"I don't believe Walter Autry had bad intentions but I know Marilyn did. She threatened me every day but I didn't let it get me down. I would focus on my children's faces and keep my hope alive that I'd get to see them again."

Shay had a picture of my children flash onto the screen behind us. "There they are, aren't they beautiful?" The audience clapped and whistled.

Shay leaned toward me and said softly, "So, now I have to ask. How are you holding up since Rusty died?"

A large picture of Rusty holding a trophy from his last race flashed on the screen. Seeing him and knowing that was right before he died, brought tears to my eyes.

"Shay, I'm doing the best I can. As you probably know, I was pregnant with Madison when his accident occurred. Going through the rest of my pregnancy without him was hard but I had a wonderful support system of friends who helped me get through it."

She handed me a tissue and took one for herself. Dabbing her eyes she said, "I can't imagine what you've gone through…and all alone."

This was it, my chance to set the record straight. "Actually, I wasn't completely alone. In my position, you have to surround yourself with people you trust and who you know have your back. I have a very special friend who has been with me through everything. He was there for me when I lost Rusty, helping me keep my focus on my son and my unborn child. When I went into labor, he was there holding my hand and coaching me until my beautiful Madison was born."

Shay looked to the audience. "This sounds like an amazing guy. Wouldn't you agree?"

The audience clapped their approval and so I continued, "Sometimes in life, you take people around you

296

for granted and end up pushing them out of your life without regard for how crappy it'll make your life. That's exactly what I did. I pushed this wonderful man from my life and instantly regretted it. He'd become so much more to me than a friend and I didn't realize it until he'd gone. Thank God he still cared about me because he was the person who rescued me from my kidnappers."

The crowd gasped and Shay's mouth fell open. "He was the one who saved you?"

I nodded. "He didn't give up until he followed every lead and finally tracked me down. He was able to subdue both of the kidnappers and bring me safely back to my children and my family."

Shay shook her head with amazement. "I can't imagine how relieved you must have been to see him."

"I'll be honest, it made me realize how much I cared for him, how much I love him." The audience grew quiet so I continued, "I know that in society, a widow is looked upon as a broken woman, her heart irreparably torn into pieces. Well, my heart *was* broken but he helped heal it. His unconditional support brought me back to life and despite what's acceptable or proper, I've fallen in love with this wonderful man."

You could hear a pin drop in the studio. Shay had tears streaming down her cheeks. She grasped my hand tightly. "I'm so happy for you. Were you afraid to tell the public about the two of you?"

"Shay, when Rusty and I said our vows, we said we'd love each other as long as we both lived but you never expect when you say it that the one you love will be taken at such a young age. I feel very blessed that I've been lucky enough to find love twice."

Shay smiled. "So, Ryanne, can you tell us more about this wonderful man?"

"Well, his name is Mason Leffler and he's here with me today. He's a former police officer who is also in charge of my personal security."

Shay waved to someone off the stage and a moment later, the crowd erupted in applause. I turned to see Mason reluctantly walking out onto the stage waving to the crowd. He perched himself on the arm of the chair then draped his arm around my shoulders. Shay stared wordlessly then finally composed herself.

"Um, are you saying he's your bodyguard?" she asked as she fanned herself with her index cards.

Mason answered for me. "Yes, ma'am. I'm in charge of her, day...and night."

My face flushed then I began to laugh when I saw Shay's cheeks turn crimson as well. "Well, I think I'd better hire a bodyguard ASAP! Wouldn't you want one if he looked like that?" she asked the audience and received a roar of applause as an answer.

"So, Mason...may I call you Mason?" Shay asked as she batted her eyelashes.

He grinned. "Yes, you can call me Mason."

"Mason, are there others like you? How do I hire a bodyguard?"

He laughed. "Yes, as a matter of fact you can contact Solitaire Security in Charlotte, North Carolina."

Shay blushed. "Are they all as hot as you?"

Mason just laughed and then the producer signaled to Shay to wrap up the segment.

"Well, folks. I have to say that I admire my friend Ryanne for following her heart and I need to get to a phone quick so I can order a bodyguard."

The crowd cheered and Shay hugged me and then Mason. "Thank you both for coming and being so open about your relationship. There are probably a lot of women who feel the same way you do but won't let the world know they've found love again. They need to know that it's okay."

Mason stood and held out his hand to me and we walked off the set hand in hand to roaring applause and cheers.

The rest of the day was pretty much a repeat of Shay's show with the exception of the hosts having more and more information about Mason. They'd obviously been interested in his background and dug deeper into his connection to the Leffler fortune. They'd also gotten in touch with Kristin but surprisingly, she'd been kind in her recollection of their marriage. When we arrived at

Rowan's interview, the makeup artists worked on both of us because obviously, she fully intended for him to be a part of the entire segment.

"Are you okay with all this?" I asked as my nose was powdered for what seemed like the fiftieth time.

He laughed. "I'd better start getting used to it."

Once we were ready for camera, we were escorted to the set of Star Spotlight. The host Rowan Harrison was highly respected by celebrities for her compassionate and in-depth interviews.

She greeted us with a hug and invited us to sit on the overstuffed couch that matched her chair. There was no live audience for this interview, just the three of us and the cameras.

"Ryanne, I want you to know that if any question makes you uncomfortable and you don't wish to answer, just let me know. I want this to be your safe space."

"Thank you, Rowan." Mason reached over and took my hand then gave it a reassuring squeeze.

Rowan turned to the camera. "Tonight, we are joined by Ryanne Charles. As you know, she is the star of many very successful movies, most recently "War of Love". She's been through a lot lately and tonight, we'll get to talk to her about her recent experiences." She turned to me and smiled. "Welcome, Ryanne."

"Thank you for having me."

"I know the last year has been a difficult one for you. Let's start with the loss of your husband. First of all, let me offer my condolences to you and your family."

"I appreciate that. It's definitely been a tough time. Everyone says that when you're the wife of a race car driver, you know that every time he goes on the track, there's a chance he won't come back. That's not true. I believed he was safer on the track than anywhere else and it turns out I was right."

Rowan nodded sympathetically. "I can't imagine what you were feeling when you found out."

"I—I couldn't breathe. It was as if someone had sucked all of the air from the room. I fainted and when I woke up, Mason was standing over me and he calmed me down."

"So, Mason's been with you for a while, as your security, I assume?" she asked.

"Yes, he was assigned to my family last year. Rusty traveled a lot and so we needed a full-time guard. Mason was really good with Gage, my son, which was important because we wanted him to feel safe. He traveled with me to Wilmington last year when we filmed the movie and we were days from wrapping it up when Rusty died."

"Mason, let me ask you. What were those days like after the accident?"

He paused to look at me then said, "Horrible. I was a police officer and I've had to inform families of accident victims many times but this was especially hard because of Ryanne being pregnant with Madison. When I got the call, I dreaded her hearing that news more than anything in my life. She's an amazing person and it killed me inside knowing the pain she was going to have to endure. I've always admired her."

"Mason, I have to ask. You've had feelings for her for a long time?"

"To be completely honest, yes. We have been good friends from the beginning and I always had the utmost respect for Rusty as both a husband and father. After he died and in the months after the accident, Ryanne and I became closer. Being with her for Madison's birth was one of the most amazing things I've ever done." He let go of my hand and slid his arm around my shoulder. "I never really came out and told her how I felt. I think it just became obvious when we were together that it was more than a job for me."

"So, Ryanne, when did you know he was someone you could see a future with?"

I hesitated because I knew that I should ignore the question and move on but my head and my mouth weren't on the same page. "We were in Los Angeles for the premiere of "War of Love" and…we had a major difference of opinion about something so he quit and left me. It was so devastating to find out the next morning that he was gone and that I had a new security guard. He left without an explanation, without a goodbye and I knew right then he meant more to me than I was willing to admit." Mason's eyes never left my face and I saw a tear form in the corner of his eye. "On top of that, I received a very threatening letter and was so alarmed by it I immediately flew back to Charlotte so I could make sure my family was safe."

"Mason, why did you leave?" Rowan asked.

He sighed. "I knew that I needed to get away. My feelings were starting to cloud my judgment in my job and I knew someone else would do a better job."

"So, you worked with Senator Fleming's son. I understand that he'd been threatened and you were his protection."

"That's correct but as soon as I found out Ryanne had been sent a threatening letter, I tried to involve myself with the team and at the same time, make sure she was safe."

"Ryanne, how in the world did you end up in the hands of the people who threatened you? It was as if you walked into their trap."

I groaned. "Well, in a nutshell, I'm an idiot. After I came back from California, I became depressed because I didn't have Mason to talk to anymore. I felt such a loss and I'd already endured so much already that it became unbearable. I retreated into my bedroom and then eventually, into my closet. There, surrounded by Rusty's personal things, I had a reckoning. It was as if Rusty were telling me to get myself together and move on. I was so excited to tell Mason how I felt that I dashed over to his apartment but unfortunately he was—"

"Having a heated discussion with my ex-wife," Mason finished.

I shrugged. "Yeah, I misunderstood the entire conversation and with my feelings all mixed up, I drove to the nearest parking lot, pulled in and within a few minutes, I'd been whacked in the head and when I woke up, I was tied up in a dingy little trailer."

"Mason, how did you react when you found out she was missing?"

Mason took a deep breath. "I can't describe the feeling. It nearly drove me insane. There's such a feeling of regret…that if something horrible has happened to her, I'd never get to tell her how much I loved her."

Tears welled in my eyes as I watched him struggle to remain composed. I squeezed his hand tightly.

"I was so desperate to find her and when I finally got the lead that I felt might pan out, I acted on it, on my own. I knew precious time was passing and if I waited for back-up, it could end up being too late."

Rowan nodded and then turned to the camera. "We'll be back with more from Ryanne Charles and Mason Leffler in just a moment."

The camera light went out and Rowan stood. "I think the interview is going really great. I'm going to let you guys have a break for about thirty minutes and then we'll finish. Feel free to go back to the green room and relax for a bit."

We stood and walked hand in hand back to the empty green room. Mason shut the door and took me into his arms. "My God, I need to do this." We silently stood holding on to each other. Finally, he eased his hold on me and looked me in the eyes. "How are you holding up?"

"I'm doing okay. It's so easy to talk to Rowan and tell her things you wouldn't be able to say comfortably. We really haven't talked about all this and I'm glad we're doing it now."

Mason ran his fingers through his hair. "I guess you sometimes need someone to coax it out of you. One of my faults is that I'm just not comfortable talking about my feelings."

I kissed him tenderly. "I don't believe you have any faults. You are one of the kindest, most caring men I've ever known. I'm so lucky to have you."

"I'm the lucky one. Ryanne, I love you and I know this is too soon, but one day, I want to marry you. I'm laying it out there and when you're ready, just let me know and I'm yours."

I slipped my hands around his waist and pulled him to me. "Thank you for giving me time," I whispered.

A moment later, a knock on the door called us back to the set. Rowan had freshened up and was waiting for us on the set. We sat back down and she began the second part of the interview.

"Welcome back. Ryanne, I'd like to ask you, how do you have the strength to carry on after all that you've been through?"

I thought for a moment and suddenly had to blink back tears. "Truthfully, I don't know. The only answer has to be for my children. Gage is a beautiful, bright child who has me wrapped around his finger and Madison is a beauty with a smile that lights up a room. They are my reason for living."

Rowan placed her hand on mine. "That's so beautiful."

"Mason, you were there when Madison was born. What were your thoughts that day?"

"Well, it was bittersweet. I got to witness to the birth of a healthy baby but her dad wasn't there and it was so sad. Also, I had to reconcile the fact that Ryanne wasn't my wife and Madison wasn't my child. It was difficult dealing with so many emotions that day but I'm thankful I was a part of it. I'll never forget the experience."

"Mason, I know this is a very personal question and feel free to tell me if you don't want to answer. Did you ever imagine you'd be in a relationship with Ryanne Charles?"

He paused and what he said next was a complete surprise to me. "Honestly? I had a crush on her after I saw her first movie. She was so beautiful and an extremely talented actress and I fell in love just like the rest of America did. Now, was this just a fantasy thing? Sure. I was a cop living in Los Angeles and was happily married. I never in my wildest dreams thought I'd ever meet her, let alone be her personal security. I guess you could say I've always been in love with her but it was the kind of love where you admire the strength and the inner goodness of someone and wish you could have someone like that in your life."

"So, when did you divorce? Was it amicable?"

He smiled. "It was before I moved to Charlotte and I'll say yes. We both wanted it and it was the best thing we ever did."

"Well, I want to wish the two of you the best. Not everyone gets another chance at love and from watching you today, I can see it's there. I hope you'll keep me updated on your relationship because I really do care and I know that your fans do too. Thank you for joining us."

The camera light went out and we were done. When we left the back door of the studio, there were several fans milling around and as soon as they spotted us, they began to cheer.

"We love you, Ryanne!"

I shook hands and signed some autographs and even posed for pictures. The day had been busy and it finally caught up with me. I was exhausted and ready to head back to the room.

Mason hailed our driver who drove us back to the hotel. In the car, we sat in silence. I was feeling so overwhelmed by everything that had happened and needed to process it. Mason had opened his heart to me today and some of it had really surprised me. He'd also proposed, in a way. I wasn't ready for that step yet but knowing that it was on his mind and a possibility for the future made me feel secure.

Back in our room, he poured us both a glass of wine and carried them to the terrace where I was sitting watching the lights come on in the buildings nearby. "So, I'm sure you're pretty wiped out."

I stifled a yawn. "It was a pretty emotional day. Tomorrow is when I'll see if all this paid off. I want people to realize that I'm a human too and I deserve happiness."

He set our glasses down then came around behind me and he began to massage my shoulders. All the stress of the day melted away under his strong hands.

"Mmm, that feels so good," I groaned.

He leaned in and kissed the side of my neck. "How's that?" he whispered.

I leaned into him. "Amazing."

He nibbled on my earlobe sending tingles all over my body. "And that?"

I turned and captured his lips with mine. We shared a slow, sweet kiss that made my heart begin to race. Without breaking our kiss, he moved to kneel in front of me and I slid my hands into his hair pulling his ponytail free. His hair tumbled to his shoulders and eagerly, I wrapped my fingers into it pulling him into a deeper kiss.

Without saying a word, I stood and pulled him to his feet then led him to the bedroom. This time there was no desperation and no confusion. I wanted him and from the look in his eyes, he felt the same.

With both hands, he cupped my face, gently feathering kisses along my jaw then down to the hollow of my neck. My breath was coming in short bursts. "I want you, Mason," I moaned, my voice husky with desire.

"Easy, baby. I'm in charge." With hooded eyes, he began to unbutton my silk blouse until my lacy bra was exposed. His wanting eyes devoured me and he groaned as he began to pepper my bare skin with soft kisses.

My hands found the buttons of his shirt and I was able to reveal his exquisite chest. I trailed my fingers through his chest hair then eased his shirt from his shoulders letting it drop to the floor. His hands slipped under my blouse, his skin warm against mine. With deft hands, he unbuttoned my skirt letting it sink to the floor where it pooled around my ankles. Mason smiled. "Baby, you are so sexy."

I felt sexy. When we'd been together before, I'd just been focused on easing my loneliness and need to feel something, anything. This time was so different. This time, I could feel the love between us.

Slowly and deliberately, he slid the rest of my clothes from my body until I was bare. The breeze from the open window danced across my skin causing me to shiver. Mason smiled then eased me down onto the bed. "I never thought I'd feel this way again," I gasped as he moved his lips across my body.

"Ryanne, my goal is to make you happy every day for the rest of your life." He captured my mouth with his and our bodies and souls became one.

Chapter 19

Mason

Once we returned from New York, things got crazy. Several magazines contacted Ryanne about doing stories on finding love after tragedy as well as more talk shows. One thing I focused on was making the kids feel more comfortable with me being around. When Ryanne was busy with meetings at the house, I'd take them to the park or we'd just go down to the pier and I worked with Gage on his fishing skills. Madison would nap in her stroller as we'd sit quietly waiting for the big one. I loved being with them and more especially with their mother who I was falling in love with more every day.

A couple of hectic months passed and then one morning, I was putting the breakfast dishes in the dishwasher when I heard Ryanne come in the kitchen. She wrapped her arms around me and lay her head against my back. "Thank you for being so wonderful."

"My pleasure," I said twisting around to face her then kissing her lightly on her lips. "So, what do you have in mind for today? You promised you'd pick something for us to do as a family."

She smiled. "I want to drive to Myrtle Beach."

"The beach? That's almost a four hour ride! This was supposed to be a day thing."

"Well, I've actually made reservations at a beach house for a week. My agent called and said I have a break between projects. I thought it would be a great time to get away. I gave Mrs. Jamison a week off so we have the kids all to ourselves."

I pulled her to me. "Sounds wonderful. You don't have to convince me, I'm just surprised, that's all."

"I've already packed for us so all you need to do is load the luggage and the kids in the truck." She turned and flounced out of the room with a satisfied smile on her face.

"Did you pack my mankini?" I called out and in reply, I heard a very wicked laugh.

In the foyer, the luggage was standing by the door so I carefully packed the vehicle and made sure that the kids would have access to their snacks and had plenty of movies to watch.

After making sure everyone was safely buckled in, we headed down to the coast.

Ryanne had found a two-story home only steps from the white sand. It had its own swimming pool and porches facing the ocean with spectacular views. We unloaded the kids and got everything put into their rooms. Gage was bouncing up and down with excitement because he saw someone flying a kite on the beach. To my surprise, Ryanne took my bags into the master bedroom. When I gave her a questioning look, she simply said, "It's time." We changed into our swim suits (no mankini) and made our way down to the water. Ryanne sat Madison on a blanket under an umbrella and she happily watched Gage try to build a sandcastle with me.

It was amazing being away from the chaos of everyday life. Ryanne had instructed Kimberly to handle everything for her unless it was literally life or death. The kids were so thrilled to have us to themselves. We loved walking down the beach feeling the surf lapping at our toes. Madison was usually perched on my shoulders with her fingers tightly clutching my hair and Gage was happily searching for shells which he carefully dropped in his bright red bucket. At night, after the kids were safely in bed, we'd sit on the balcony listening to the gentle roar of the surf against the sand.

One night after we'd made love, we lay wrapped in each other's arms and she began to cry softly.

"Baby? What's wrong?" I asked wiping the tear rolling down her cheek away. She was quiet and it began to scare me. I tipped her chin to make her look me in the eyes. "Ryanne?"

"I'll be okay, I'm just really happy," she whispered.

I wrapped her in my arms and held her tight until we drifted off to sleep.

The week flew by and soon it was time to head back to reality. We all had such a wonderful time and I felt it really brought us closer together. We packed up the kids and headed back to our chaotic life.

As soon as we arrived, Kimberly deluged Ryanne with requests for appearances on several different talk shows but she quickly dismissed them. She was satisfied she'd said all she needed to.

We fell into a routine of spending time with the kids and stealing moments alone. One added bonus of all the media hype was that she was offered the lead role in several projects. A major fragrance manufacturer offered her a very lucrative contract to create and market her own perfume. She was so excited and very pleased to be able to pick and choose her projects.

I was able to keep myself busy with planning the security for her trips and also keeping tabs on the house and the kids. One thing always on my mind was my unanswered proposal. I don't know why it bothered me so badly because we were living as if we were married already but I really wanted her to be mine in every way and that hadn't happened yet.

One afternoon, Ryanne was going to be tied up at the house with meetings so I decided to take the kids out for ice cream. I was buckling Gage into his booster seat and heard a car pull into the driveway. I peered around the door and saw Lucas climb from his Range Rover.

"Hey, Mason!" He called out with a wave. He came over and stuck his head in the car. "What's up, kiddos? Where are y'all going?"

Gage grinned and said, "Ice cream!"

Madison, who was trying to copy everything her brother said came up with, "Baabbbaaa!"

Lucas laughed and patted them both on the legs. "Well, y'all have fun. I'm jealous." He made a sad face and they both giggled. After I shut the door, Lucas said, "Hey, how's everything with you and Ryanne?"

Knowing he was a close friend of Rusty's I used caution when I answered. "Things are good. Just living life. You know how that is."

He nodded solemnly. "Yeah, I thought so. Look, I can see things are kinda at a standstill. You're a good guy and deserve a break. Let me see if I can help."

"Help? How?"

"I'll talk to her, see if I can find out what's holding her back," he said as he slapped me on the back. "Wish me luck."

"If you can help, I wish you all the luck in the world."

I climbed in the truck and watched him walk into the house. I'd never really talked to him before and I couldn't help but like him. He reminded me of Rusty and it was easy to see why they'd been best friends.

"Ice cream!" Gage yelled from the back seat.

"Baabbbaaa!" Madison squealed.

I pulled out of the driveway with high hopes that Lucas could bring Ryanne around.

About two hours later, we rolled back into the driveway. Gage and Madison were fast asleep after having worn themselves out at the park after our ice cream date. Gage had insisted on playing on the slide while Madison wanted to swing so they kept me busy trying to watch them both. I unbuckled Gage and he yawned sleepily and then smiled. "I had fun," he said with a grin.

"I'm glad you did. Do you want me to carry you or do you want to walk?" I asked as I unbuckled Madison.

"I'm a big boy. I can walk. I'm five!" I picked him up and set him on the driveway then scooped the still sleeping princess from the car seat. As we walked up to the door, it opened and Lucas came out.

"Hey, kids, let me get the door for you." He held the door open and Gage bounded in. As I passed, he said, "Well, she finally opened up to me. I hope she can do the same with you."

The way he said it irked me. Why could Ryanne open up to him and not me? I followed Gage inside and found Ryanne waiting at the door. "Hey, little man, did you have fun?" she asked bending down to give him a kiss and hug.

"Yeah! Daddy took us to get ice cream!"

We both froze and looked at each other. The awkward silence was broken by Gage recounting our trip to the park. I could hardly breathe. I'd wanted to hear those words all my life and to actually hear them was like music to my ears. Gage took his mom by the hand and led

322

her upstairs. I carried the still sleeping Madison to her room and laid her down for the rest of her nap. When I came out into the hallway, Ryanne was shutting Gage's door.

She backed me into her room and shut the door. "Mason, we need to talk."

Her face didn't give any indication of what that meant so for a moment, all I could think was that Lucas was a piece of crap who was able to get the love of my life to divulge her fears and, because of his friendship with Rusty, probably sabotaged my chance at a future with Ryanne.

I dropped onto the bed and watched her pace back and forth in front of me waiting for her to speak. The longer she paced, the more anxious I became. Finally, she stopped. "I need to say something and I don't want you to say anything until I'm finished. Is that okay?"

"Um, I guess I have no choice," I said, my voice tight. My emotions were wound raw and a knot formed in my stomach as I waited to hear the fate of our relationship.

Chapter 20

Ryanne

The minute Lucas walked in, I knew he had something on his mind and was I right. He gave me a hug and a peck on the cheek then plopped down in the chair across from me. He propped his feet on the edge of the desk, tented his fingers and stared at me.

"What?" I asked with a nervous giggle.

"So, what are we going to do about Mason?" He looked up at the ceiling and sighed. "I mean, he's a really decent guy and the kids love him. What's holding you back? Be honest with me."

I sank onto the leather couch and curled my legs under me. "I don't know. Even though I've told the world that I'm ready to move on, I'm still hanging on to some doubt. I know you've said you support me and I appreciate that but I just don't know if I'd be doing the right thing."

He slid his feet to the floor and leaned toward me. "Ryanne, Rusty's gone. I miss that crazy son of a bitch every day but he's gone. One thing I do know is that he'd be sorely disappointed in the both of us. We're both clinging to the past and precious days are slipping by while we're doing it. I haven't been to a racetrack since Rusty died, I haven't been fishing…the list goes on and on. You, on the other hand, have a pretty darn good looking guy who is head over heels in love with you living under the same roof and you're afraid to take your relationship to the next level. I get it. I really do. You're afraid that if you agree to marry him," he paused and smiled at my shocked expression. "Darlin', I know he has to have asked you by now." He cleared his throat and continued, "You're afraid that you'll lose him just like Rusty. Well, let me tell you, you might as well cut him loose now and just live alone for the rest of your life because if we all waited for sure things, we'd never live."

I couldn't look him in the eye. He'd hit the nail on the head and it stung to hear it said out loud. I didn't want to cut Mason loose. I loved him. "Lucas, I know I've probably ruined things by dragging this out with him. Do you think he still wants to marry me?"

He leaned back and laughed. "Are you kidding? The man is totally in. I guarantee if you asked him today, he'd be picking out the china by this afternoon."

I laughed. Lucas was right. Mason would be totally on board. It was time to take a step forward instead of standing still. "Thank you for being so frank with me. I needed that." Tears sprang to my eyes.

He stood and pulled me to my feet. Wrapping his arms around me, he pulled me into a tight hug. "You're family to me and I don't want my family hurtin'."

He released me from the hug, wiped the tears from my eyes and kissed my forehead. "Now, I want you to clean yourself up and go propose to that poor man. Make yourselves happy."

He looked over my shoulder at the monitor for the security and smiled. "Looks like your family just came home. I'll stall Mason while you go freshen up."

I turned and ran into the small bathroom by the kitchen and splashed water on my face.

When I saw Mason, all the confidence I'd built up from talking to Lucas went right out the window and doubt crept back into my mind. There was no doubt about what I should do, but I had serious doubt that he'd still want me.

Then I got thrown off by Gage. When he said that Daddy had taken him for ice cream, my heart literally jumped in my chest. He didn't even seem to realize what he'd said so obviously, he felt completely comfortable saying it.

When I looked at Mason for his reaction, I saw the hint of a smile but then it quickly disappeared. I made my mind up right then that we needed to talk as soon as possible. It was time to lay my fears on the table.

After Gage and Madison were down for their naps, I took the opportunity to pull Mason into the bedroom. My thoughts were jumbled and I didn't know where to start. When I asked if I could say what I needed to without interruption, I saw him tense up and that made me even more apprehensive.

"Mason, I–" I paused and took a deep breath. "I was talking to Lucas and…"

He held up his hand. "I know you said you don't want to be interrupted but I have to ask, how could you tell him how you felt? Do you know how that makes me feel?"

He was angry. I could feel it. "It's not like that. He backed me into a corner."

"So, all along I just needed to put pressure on you? I've been trying to give you time to heal and find yourself again but instead, I should have forced you to tell me how you feel?"

I felt my face flush. He was right. He'd been so supportive and never pressured me and all it did was let me keep my fears locked inside. "Mason, you've been so great…"

He stood and I took a step back. "Look, I'm not in the right frame of mind to hear this right now. I need some air." He walked past me and out the door.

I bit my lip to keep from bursting into tears. This was not how it was supposed to go. I buried my face in my hands and tried to gather my thoughts. As I took my hands away, I glanced out the bedroom window and saw him walking down the pier to the lake. He was running his hands through his hair and pacing up and down, obviously agitated. It was time to be strong and tell him exactly what my heart wanted.

I ran downstairs and out to the dock. By the time I got there, he'd stopped pacing and was now sitting on the edge with his back to me. His shoulders were tense and he was clenching and unclenching his fists. Just seeing how upset he was brought tears to my eyes. I walked up behind him, took a deep breath and finally let him in.

"I'm scared," I whispered. "Everything's so perfect and I'm afraid something bad is going to happen. I really do love you."

He turned slowly.

"I'm so sorry, I should've told you how I felt."

He sighed. "You have every right to be scared. Life's kicked you pretty hard and you've been just waiting for the next blow." His expression softened. "Ryanne, a lot of people feel the same way after a tragedy."

I sat down beside him and placed my hand over his. "Mason, after Rusty died, my heart was shattered and I never thought it would heal. You fixed me by being patient with me and showing me that it was okay to love again."

He leaned toward me and kissed me softly. "I'm the luckiest man on earth." He held me tightly.

"I don't deserve to be this happy," I whispered against his ear. "God has blessed me twice in a lifetime and I'm so thankful. I'm ready to live again."

He took my hands and brought them to his lips. "I love you, Ryanne."

I looked into his eyes. "Mason, will you marry me?"

He smiled. "Yes, Ryanne, yes with all my heart."

He stood and pulled me to my feet. "I know that this is supposed to be official with a ring…"

I laughed. "Well, you can't be expected be carrying one around on the off chance I'd propose."

He nodded. "You're right. But…" He reached in his pants pocket and pulled out a ring box. "I'm not just anyone."

My eyes grew wide and my mouth fell open with surprise. "What? You're kidding me!"

He cracked the box open and dropped to one knee. "I would never kid about the most important moment of my life. Ryanne, make me the happiest man on earth and please accept this ring as a promise that I will love and protect you for the rest of our lives."

He held up the box to reveal a solitaire with a soft pink stone. "When I started my ring search, I wanted the perfect ring for the perfect woman. The stone needed to have meaning for the both of us. This is Kunzite, a beautiful crystal, pure in energy. I was told by the jeweler that it encourages the wearer to release walls built around the heart for protection and to be receptive to the experience of unconditional and abundant love. It also symbolizes eternal love. It's the perfect stone for us."

I blinked back tears as he pulled the ring from the box and slipped it onto my finger. "Mason, you're right, it is perfect," I gasped.

He kissed the ring then stood and kissed me. I wrapped my arms around him and held him tight. He lifted me off my feet and swung me around. "I love you, baby," he whispered in my ear. He set me on my feet and then raised his eyes to the sky and whispered, "I promise."

That simple gesture touched my heart so much that I thought I'd burst with happiness. We locked hands and walked back to the house to begin sharing the news.

Everyone was thrilled to hear that we were going to get married and even though the kids didn't really know what that meant, they were happy that Mason was with us and we were a family.

Chapter 21

Mason

Weddings take time to plan but ours came together in record time. Two months later, the afternoon of the wedding finally arrived and all day it had been utter chaos downstairs. I leaned over the railing to see the wedding planner running around barking orders to those with a specific job to do like a drill sergeant. The caterer was directing her people and the florist was quietly carrying in the ornate flower arrangements. It was really interesting to watch since I'd pretty much left all the decisions to Ryanne and her matron of honor, Jolene.

Ryanne and I had been sharing a room since the beach trip but I'd insisted that the night before the wedding, I would sleep in my room to keep up tradition. I went back into my room and grabbed a shower then as I was dressing, I heard a knock at the door.

"Yo, Mason! It's Ryder!"

"Come on in," I shouted as I searched for a stray cuff link.

Ryder opened the door and I saw he was already dressed. "Looking good, man. You clean up nice."

"Thanks, I try," I chuckled.

"So, are you getting nervous?" he asked picking up the cuff link from the floor beside the bed. "I know I was."

"You? Nervous? No way. You absolutely adore Jolene. I can't see you being nervous."

Ryder nodded solemnly. "Yes, I was nervous. Not about marrying the woman I've loved all my life but about messing up what I wanted to say. It's scary as hell knowing everyone is hanging on your every word, especially your bride."

Suddenly, sweat popped out on my forehead. "Damn, I was pretty calm until you said that," I groaned. I picked up the paper I'd written my vows on and studied them closely. "I hope I don't screw this up."

Ryder laughed and clapped me on the shoulder. "It'll be okay. Don't try to memorize it word for word. If you do, you'll sound like a robot. Just say what's in your heart and you'll be just fine."

I took a deep breath and sighed. "I can do this. I've dreamed of this day for a long time."

Ryder checked my tie and helped me fasten the rogue cufflink. He brushed my shoulders off and gave me a thumbs up. "I think it's just about that time."

I followed Ryder down the stairs and out into the yard where we had tents set up for the ceremony. The tents were necessary to keep the paparazzi from flying over in helicopters trying to get photos. We'd chosen the same spot that Ryder and Jolene's wedding had been held. An arbor was set up using the lake as a background. The final guests were being seated and I felt a rush of adrenaline knowing we were just moments away from the wedding. Mr. West the minister joined Ryder and me and escorted us out to the arbor where we took our places. I smiled looking around at all the wonderful people who'd come to share our special day with us. Ryanne's parents were seated in front of Rusty's parents who had been thrilled to attend. Both couples had accepted me completely easing any anxiety I might have had about my role in Ryanne's life.

The music began and Gage began to make his way down the aisle with Madison. He was pulling her in a wagon and she was giggling all the way. When they reached the end of the aisle, Cara picked Madison up to set her on her knee. Gage climbed up onto the chair next to her and gave me a big grin.

Jolene came down the aisle next wearing a beautiful lavender strapless gown that she'd designed herself for the wedding. Her eyes locked with Ryder's and she gave him a sweet smile and blew him a kiss.

My palms grew sweaty as the anticipation of seeing Ryanne grew. The music changed to signal the entrance of the bride and the guests stood as Ryanne, escorted by her father, started down the aisle.

Literally, I lost my breath. She was stunning. Our eyes locked and all the anxiety went away followed by a sense of calm. When she finally stood beside me my hands were trembling as I held out my arm to escort her to the altar. She was wearing an off-white satin strapless gown that fit her body like a glove, which was also custom designed by Jolene. Her jewelry was simple, a single strand of pearls along with tiny pearl stud earrings. Her blonde hair was pulled into a loose braid which hung over her shoulder. I was a goner.

"Friends, family and guests," Mr. West began. "We're gathered here today to bring two very special people together in marriage. Today we are celebrating a new beginning for Ryanne and Mason. This is an important step for them both as they begin a life together as man and wife and also as a family with Gage and Madison. They ask you pray for them as they begin this journey."

He allowed a moment of prayer then continued, "Ryanne and Mason are a lovely couple who have faced many challenges in their lives that will shape the relationship to come. They want you to know that they are happy to share this moment with you. They have known most of you for several years. You have watched them grow up, you went to school with them, or you worked

337

with them. Because you are the ones who have supported them and known them so well, it is only fitting that you are the ones to share this moment with them. When Ryanne and Mason wrote their vows, they reflected on what they love most about each other and they'd like to share that with you now."

I cleared my throat and looked into Ryanne's eyes. "Ryanne, I know I've said this many times but I love everything about you. That means I love that you are a great mom, a talented actress, a smart businesswoman, an okay fisherman, and a great friend to everyone you meet. I promise that I will be a faithful and loving husband forever."

Ryanne dabbed her eyes with a tissue and began her vows. "Mason, you're such a special man. You've seen me at my worst and you've stood by my side and supported me through all the turmoil in my life. My children love you and it's obvious that you love them just as much. My heart is yours if you'll have it. Also, I think you'd better stick around and give me some fishing lessons." I laughed and everyone joined in. She continued, "I promise I won't take you for granted, that you will laugh a lot and that we'll grow older and wiser together."

Mr. West nodded with a smile. "Beautiful, just beautiful. Now, the rings. Gage, can you bring me the pillow that's in the wagon?" Gage scrambled off of his chair, scooped up the pillow and held it up. The minister laughed. "Can you bring it to your mommy? Please?"

He carried it to Ryanne and as she bent down to get it, she whispered, "That's my big boy!" He was beaming as he ran back to join his grandparents who were obviously proud of his job. Ryanne passed the pillow to Mr. West, who untied the bands from it.

"These rings," he said holding them up, "are symbols of eternity, with no beginning or end. The hole in the center of the ring symbolizes a gateway or door leading to things and events both known and unknown. The exchange of rings signifies never-ending and immortal love."

He handed Ryanne's ring to me and as I slipped it on her finger, I said, "I give you this ring as a symbol of my undying love for you. As this ring has no end, my love is also forever."

She took my ring from him and as she slipped it on my finger, she said, "With this ring, I give you my heart. It is yours forever."

Mr. West placed his hands on our shoulders, said a blessing then pronounced us married. "You may now kiss your wife."

I pulled Ryanne into my arms and kissed her softly and I could hear sniffles from several of the guests. I took her by the hand and we took our first steps as man and wife.

The reception was held in another tent at the other end of the yard. As we entered the tent, we were met with a rousing round of applause and whistles. Tables were lined along the walls of the tent and in the center they'd set up a dance floor. At the end of the tent, Lucas had set up with his band. He'd generously agreed to be our entertainment and for our first dance, he'd picked a special song just for us.

We made our way to the center of the dance floor and the music began. Lucas strummed his guitar and as he did, we swayed to the music. I recognized the song immediately. It was one of my favorites. "From This Moment" by Shania Twain was the perfect choice.

There wasn't a dry eye in the place. As our song ended, I pulled Ryanne tightly to me and whispered, "I love you so much."

With tears glistening in her eyes, she whispered back, "I love you too."

We opened up the dance floor to everyone else and the party really began. Ryder and Jolene encouraged people to get out and join us. Gage became the center of the attention when he started dancing and Madison clapped and giggled watching her brother do his thing. Darryl had brought a date but seemed to be ignoring her and was instead in a serious discussion with Lucinda, Jolene's best friend from England. Joey and Olivia had started out dancing but soon disappeared with a bottle of champagne in hand much to our amusement. We danced until we literally couldn't dance anymore and the party began to wind down. Ryanne and I were going to be honeymooning at home with the kids and looking forward to every minute of it. I'd bought a pontoon boat and we loved putt putting around the lake and teaching the kids to swim. Our plan was to use plenty of sunscreen and get as much fresh air as possible before Ryanne's next project which was the starring role in a movie based on a best-selling romance novel.

The last of the guests departed and I scooped my bride into my arms and carried her up the stairs to our room. Pushing the door shut with my foot, I turned and deposited her on the bed. I threw myself down beside her and pulled her close.

"I can't wait to make love to you, Mrs. Leffler," I whispered as I feathered kisses along her cheek.

She moaned and lifted her chin to allow me to travel along the curve of her neck. "I'm all yours," she whispered. "Forever…"

Epilogue

Mason

"Maci! Come back here!" I yelled as I chased my eighteen month old daughter across the yard. "We've got to get going, Mommy's waiting!"

"Did she ditch her clothes again?" Ryanne called as she came out of the house with Gage and Madison.

"Yes, she's definitely happier with a bare butt," I laughed. I caught up with her and scooped her into my arms. "You silly little bug," I said as I peppered her face with kisses.

When I got to the truck, the kids were already buckled in and ready to go. I dressed Maci quickly and then strapped her in her car seat. "Okay are we ready to go?" I asked.

"Yes! Let's go!" Gage shouted.

We drove to the local party store and picked out a dozen balloons of assorted colors and stuffed them into the back of the truck. When we arrived at the park, Gage was out of his seat and ready to go. I opened the door for him and he quickly unbuckled Madison while I grabbed Maci. With the balloons in tow, we made our way to the large grassy area where most people threw Frisbees and played catch. Gage solemnly held the balloons while his sisters watched fascinated.

"Okay, on the count of three we're sending these to Heaven," he said looking skyward.

"One, two, three!" He let the strings go and the balloons drifted into the sky. We watched them go higher and higher until we couldn't see them anymore. "Dad, do you think he'll like the different colors this time?" Gage asked as we walked back to the playground in the park. It never ceased to amaze me when he called me dad. It was so effortless with Madison since I was the only dad she knew, but Gage had known his father and on his own had adjusted to our new family dynamic.

I ruffled his hair. "Yes, I really think he will. You did a good job."

With a grin, he ran over to climb the slide. Madison backed up to a swing then smiled as Ryanne pushed it to make her go.

"Whee!" she squealed. "Faster, Mommy! Faster!"

Maci, who was in my arms, was struggling to get free so she could join in the fun. I slipped her into the baby swing and pushed her gently. Her black curls bounced as she threw her head back to look at the sky. The happiness I felt at that moment was indescribable. The kids were all healthy and happy and for that I was thankful. Gage was looking so much like Rusty that it was uncanny and even some of his mannerisms were spot on. Lucas had even commented on it when he and Trina brought their little boy Tatum over for playdates.

Gage had been riding his bicycle around the yard and apparently had heard a squeak so he grabbed a wrench out of the shed and quickly dismantled it. Lucas and I were sitting on lawn chairs watching him closely and I heard Lucas remark, "You know, Rusty used to do the same exact thing." A few minutes later, Gage had the bike put back together and was happily riding squeak free.

"Hey guys!" I looked around and saw Jolene and Ryder getting out of their car. Jolene was due to deliver their baby girl any day and Ryder had been taking her out for walks to try to get her labor started.

I waved and they headed over to join us. Madison had already tired of the swing so she wandered over to take turns on the slide with Gage.

"So, how are we coming along?" Ryanne asked as Jolene dropped onto the picnic table bench.

"Slow but steady," she groaned. "The doctor says we're doing all the right things."

Ryanne sat down next to Jolene. "It's your first so everything's bound to be slower. Just hang in there. She'll be here before you know it."

She nodded and laughed as she rubbed her belly. "Yeah, I just have no patience."

She gave her a sympathetic pat on the shoulder. "So, have you heard from Olivia?"

Jolene nodded. "Yeah, she's doing great. She got my office all set up in London and as soon as I can travel again, I'm going to go over and check it out."

"So what's the latest with her and Joey?"

She shrugged. "I don't really know. They seemed to be real close then suddenly they weren't. When I ask her about it, she just changes the subject."

Ryder nodded. "Joey's being tight-lipped too."

I frowned. "That's a shame. They seemed really happy."

Ryder held out his hand to her. "Come on, beautiful. Let's walk."

She let him pull her to her feet. "Well, I guess we're off." With a wave, they began to stroll along the pathway that wound through the park.

"Hey, babe," I whispered. "Check this out."

Maci had fallen asleep in the swing so I carefully lifted her up into my arms. As I held her tightly to my chest, it reminded me of how I'd held her the day she was born.

Ryanne found out she was pregnant by accident, literally. Six months after the wedding, she was driving to meet Jolene for lunch to go over an ad campaign that they were going to be working on together and she got rear-ended by a teenager who'd been texting on her cell phone. The EMT's checked her over for injuries which, from a cursory exam, only consisted of a sore neck from the impact. They wanted to take her to the hospital just to be sure but she insisted she was fine and since the car was drivable, went on to the restaurant. While they were eating, she began to have sharp pains in her abdomen and Jolene was alarmed that she may have had some internal injuries. After calling me and telling me where to meet them, she took her to the ER and after several tests, they told her that she had a cracked rib and that she was pregnant.

I was so happy and pampered her every step of the way. When we went for the ultrasound, I held her hand and together we learned we were having a girl. We'd tossed around some names and finally agreed on Maci Anne. Her pregnancy was uneventful and on her due date, Maci came into the world. I was so excited to cut the cord and was the first one to hold her. With tears in my eyes, I said to my beautiful wife, "Thank you for my miracle."

"Penny for your thoughts," Ryanne whispered in my ear as she wrapped her arm around my waist.

"I was just thinking how wonderful our life is," I said giving her a kiss on the cheek.

She nodded. "It is pretty awesome. Babe, I want to thank you for helping all of us heal and remembering Rusty is a big part of that. You're a very special man," she said hugging me tightly.

Gage and Madison came running over to us and took our hands. "Mom…Dad, don't forget we always get ice cream!" They cried in unison.

Ryanne leaned down and hugged them to her. "We didn't forget."

They began to make their way to the truck and as I followed behind, I mentally gave thanks for my life and once again vowed to Rusty that I'd love and protect them for the rest of my life. Just then, a strong breeze blew up out of nowhere and I knew he'd heard my promise.

THE END

www.ingramcontent.com/pod-product-compliance
Lightning Source LLC
Chambersburg PA
CBHW062009170626
46813CB00001B/88

* 9 7 8 0 9 9 0 8 3 0 8 3 2 *